A QUESTION OF TRUST

ALSO BY
MARION DANE BAUER:

Ghost Eye

A QUESTION OF TRUST

MARION DANE BAUER

AN
APPLE
PAPERBACK

SCHOLASTIC INC.
New York Toronto London Auckland Sydney

No part of this publication may be reproduced in whole or in part, or stored in a retrieval system, or transmitted in any form or by any means, electronic, mechanical, photocopying, recording, or otherwise, without written permission of the publisher. For information regarding permission, write to Scholastic Inc., 555 Broadway, New York, NY 10012.

ISBN 0-590-47923-7

12 11 10 9 8 7 6 5 4 3 2 1   9   5 6 7 8 9/9 0/0

Printed in the U.S.A.   40

For the Gooderl family,
Ray, Brent, Ann, and Carolyn,
and especially in memory of Mary Alice,
because you are the ones who never went away.

ACKNOWLEDGMENTS

With thanks to L. M. Wendland, D.V.M., and Julie Smith, D.V.M., for confirming my medical facts. And thanks, too, to librarians everywhere, but especially those at the Eden Prairie Center Community Library of Eden Prairie, Minnesota, for being a constant source of support and information.

A QUESTION OF TRUST

CHAPTER ONE

The telephone was ringing. A distant trill floated out through the screened patio door, traveled the length of the backyard, and burrowed into Brad's brain. Still, he made no move toward the house. It was the eighth ring — surely she would give up soon — and he sat on a swing of the rusty play set watching his younger brother out of the corner of his eye. If Charlie made a dash toward the phone, Brad would tackle him. After all, hadn't they agreed?

But Charlie wasn't moving, either. He sat scuffing the soft dust beneath his swing, his lower lip caught between his teeth, humming something tuneless beneath his breath. He was, Brad knew, trying to block out the insistent ringing.

Well, that was all right. Charlie was eight years old, but he was still pretty much a mommy's boy. Their mother's leaving, moving to her own apartment, was probably harder on him than it was on anyone else. Dad could go off to his office in the basement to work and forget all of them. Brad could stay angry. Good and angry. But Charlie had gone quiet, except for when he was alone in his bed at night. Then he cried. He wasn't quiet about that. And every night Brad heard Dad shuffle down the hallway to Charlie's room, heard his voice rumbling, low and reassuring. It was almost enough to make Brad wish he weren't twelve and too old for crying. Almost.

The ringing stopped, finally. How many times had it been? Twelve? Fifteen? He had lost count. The silence that followed was, itself, a noise, a pressure inside his skull.

"That'll teach her," Charlie said, giving the ground beneath his swing a vicious kick that sent up a cloud of dust. But despite the tough tone, the blue eyes he turned on Brad were too brilliant to be entirely dry.

"Yeah." Brad gave Charlie an encouraging thump on the back. "That'll teach her. We told her we'd be busy."

Charlie was silent for a moment. "Are we going to be busy next Friday, too?" he asked finally.

"And the Friday after that," Brad reminded him.

"And will she keep on calling, even if we don't answer?" Charlie began twisting his swing around and around so that the chains wound into a single strand above his head.

"You heard her," Brad said. "When I told her we'd be busy this Friday, she said she'd call the same time next Friday . . . and the one after that. She'll keep calling, wanting us to come for the weekend, until she gives up and comes home."

Charlie continued winding the swing, and Brad reached out and caught it to stop his twisting. It was crucial that Charlie understand the plan, that he stay with it. "Remember the time last year when Mom got so mad at Dad that she went to stay with Grandma? Do you remember why she came back then?"

"Why?" Charlie asked, though Brad was sure he knew. He sat hunched over, staring at the ground. The twisted chains pressed against the back of his neck.

"Because I wouldn't talk to her when she called, that's why. It made her so miserable, she couldn't stand it . . . so she came home." He released Charlie's swing, and it spun around three or four times, dropping into a forward position again with a metallic clunk.

Charlie took a quick swipe beneath his nose and peered at Brad. "And if we don't talk to her when she calls, she's gonna come home again. Right?" His eyelashes were almost embarrassingly long, curled and thick like a girl's.

Brad nodded emphatically. "If we *both* don't talk to her this time, she'll have to. She'll miss us so much, she won't have any choice."

"Yeah," Charlie agreed. "She'll really miss us." He said it bravely, but his voice faltered, still.

Brad thumped him on the back again, half reassurance, half warning. Ever since their mother had moved out five days ago, Brad'd had to work on Charlie to keep him in line. To make sure they were pulling together to bring her back home. Who ever heard of a mother leaving a perfectly good house to go off and live by herself in a crummy apartment? For that matter, who ever heard of a mother wanting "a life of my own," as though her husband and two sons were suddenly in the way after all these years? If he and Charlie went running to answer the phone every time she called, it would be like telling her that she'd been right to go and ruin their family. And they weren't about to do that. Not now or next week or ever.

"What do you want to do?" he asked Charlie. They had eaten supper early so that Dad could clear out of the kitchen before the call, and the soft summer evening spread before them, empty and somehow without possibilities.

Ordinarily Charlie would have come alive at the suggestion that Brad wanted to do something together, almost anything, but now he just shrugged and began winding his swing again.

Brad sighed. He'd had to stay here to make sure that Charlie didn't break rank and answer the phone, but he could go over to Scott's now. Except that he didn't especially feel like going over to Scott's. These days Scott was always asking questions, making comments. Like, "Is your mom really gone? When is she coming back? Is your dad pretty mad about it all? Mine would be steamed, really steamed!"

Who cared how *steamed* Scott's dad would be? Who cared about anything, really?

"Look at that skinny—fat cat," Charlie said, and Brad looked up to see a mottled creature slinking across the lawn. Charlie's description was right. The cat was skinny and fat at the same time. Her belly was bulbous, swollen into a mound on each side, but she was so thin that her hipbones were distinctly visible through her short fur.

As though she had understood Charlie's words, the cat came to a full stop and turned to stare in the boys' direction. Her pale eyes were disdainful, accusing. It was as if they were the intruders here, sitting on the rusty swing set in their own backyard.

"Ugly, isn't she?" Brad picked up a pebble from beneath his swing and tossed it in the cat's direction. The pebble fell short, and the cat didn't even blink.

She *was* ugly. Her fur was dark, a splotchy mixture of black and orange and cream. Her face was divided down the middle, half dark, half light. And when she had spotted them, she'd laid her ears back, close to her head, which gave her a fierce, almost an evil, appearance. It was clear that she wasn't friendly.

After glaring for a long minute, the cat turned and continued her progress. She had apparently decided that the boys weren't worth her concern. The points of her shoulder blades rose and fell as she made her way toward the back of the yard.

Brad watched her go. She lifted each paw and set it down delicately, deliberately, as though she were stepping between the blades of grass. At the end of the yard, she stopped in front of the old toolshed. The door stood open, and she sniffed at the entrance, then rubbed the side of her chin along the door-frame. The shed was empty, rarely used except by the boys as a kind of playhouse. Their dad didn't have very many tools, anyway, and he kept those few in the garage. He was an accountant and spent all his time in his basement office, adding other people's numbers.

"Maybe it's going to stay," Charlie said, rising and peering in the cat's direction. She stood indecisively, half in, half out of the shed. "Do you suppose Dad will let us keep it?"

"No way," Brad said. If Mom had still been at home, there might have been a chance, but Dad was the one with the long memory. If they mentioned wanting a cat, he would remember the time in third grade when Brad had brought the class mice home for Christmas vacation and forgotten to feed them. By the time the cage had been discovered under his bed, Mickey and Minnie had been cold and stiff. Or he would bring up Charlie's accidentally cooking his guppies by setting their bowl on a heat register, though Charlie must not have been more than five years old at the time.

Brad had heard their mom complain once that Dad never forgave and forgot anything. And even though it was pretty much true, they'd had a big fight when she'd said it. In any case, this wasn't exactly the right moment to start expecting their father to change.

The cat made up her mind finally and stalked into the shed as if it had been hers all along.

Charlie jumped up. "Let's go check it out." He ran on ahead, and Brad followed.

If the cat stayed, Brad had decided before he had even reached the shed, they wouldn't need to tell Dad. At least not right away. It would be better to keep her a secret until Mom came home. In the meantime, they could make friends with her, feed her, take care of her. And, then, once she really belonged to them, they could let both parents see how *responsible* they had been. If anything would convince their father, that would. That and their mother.

Charlie had stopped in the doorway and was peering into the shed. "I can't see the cat," he complained. "Where did it go?"

Brad looked over Charlie's shoulder. She had to be in there. There was no way out of the shed except through the doorway or through the small, dusty window with one pane missing. She hadn't come back through the door, and the window was set high in the wall, too high, he was sure, even for a cat to jump through. Brad moved past Charlie, but then hesitated for a moment, waiting for his eyes to adjust to the dim light. If he stepped on the cat, it might scratch or bite or even run up his leg.

The old shed was made of plywood and cedar shingles, and it was filled with the nose-tickling smell of wood and straw. The straw was left over from the archery target Mom had fixed up for them last fall when they'd been playing Robin Hood. She'd always been good at making things like that. When they'd lost all their arrows and broken the string on one bow, they'd torn the bales apart and made a nest on the floor of the shed to bury themselves in when they played winter survival. (That had been Mom's idea, too.)

A strange sound came from the deepest pile of straw in the corner, a ragged vibration that Brad couldn't quite name. "Sounds like a rattlesnake to me," he said. He knew better, of course. There were no rattlesnakes in central Minnesota. But sometimes it was fun to scare Charlie.

"A rattlesnake with hiccups," Charlie added, ignoring the taunt.

It was only the sound of purring, of course. That had to be what it was. But there was something strange about it. The heavy rhythm seemed too ragged, even too loud, for a normal purr.

"It sure is a happy cat," Charlie said, a little doubtfully.

"Happy because she's found a home," Brad agreed, eager to ease his own doubt.

Brad reached for the flashlight they always kept on the shelf inside the door and shone it in the direction of the sound. The cat was hunkered down in the straw in the corner, still purring violently. When the beam of light hit her, the noise stopped long enough for her to open her triangular pink mouth in a prolonged hiss. Then, immediately, she went back to the ragged purring again.

Brad stepped closer, his heart already sinking. Was there something wrong with the creature, alternately purring and hissing like that? He knelt down in front of her, staring into her eyes. They were the color of peeled grapes. Even as he studied her, the pupils enlarged, then narrowed into tight slits, then enlarged again as though she were studying him.

Someone must have abandoned this cat. Someone had probably just gone off somewhere and left her to fend for herself. Thinking she was ugly. Thinking a skinny–fat cat wasn't worth worrying about, anyway. Thinking of nothing except themselves and their new apartment and their new life.

"Don't worry, Cat," Brad murmured, reaching out to touch the tip of her mottled tail. "You've come to the right place."

The cat stopped purring and raked one paw across the back of his hand, claws extended.

Brad jerked his stinging hand away. "Ow!" he cried, lifting it to his mouth.

The pale green eyes remained steady on his face, boring into him. They were both pleading and fierce.

"It's okay, little cat," Brad told her, lowering his hand but staying carefully clear of the claws this time. "You don't have to be scared any more. Charlie and I'll take good care of you. And we won't ever go away and leave you, either."

CHAPTER TWO

"Let's not tell Dad, all right, Charlie?" Brad stood and backed away as he spoke. "We'll let Cat be our secret. At least for now."

"Is that what you're going to call it?" Charlie asked, sounding doubtful. "Just Cat? Mom would be able to think up a better name than that."

Brad couldn't help being annoyed. Charlie was right, of course. Mom could always think up names, neat things to do, even unusual excuses for staying up past bedtime or missing an occasional day of school. But what difference did any of that make now? "Well, Mom's not here. Remember? And I could think up a better name, too, if she was enough of a cat to deserve something better. I mean, look at her. She's ugly and she might even be sick, too."

"Yeah," Charlie said softly, but Brad didn't know

if he was agreeing that the cat was ugly and sick, or if he was just saying *yes, I remember that Mom isn't here.*

Charlie asked next, "Why are you calling it a she? It might be a boy cat."

"It might," Brad agreed. "I guess I just think of all cats as girls. Sneaky, you know."

"They're soft, though." Tears threatened at the edges of Charlie's words. "And they're — "

"Not much loyalty, either," Brad interrupted. "Not like dogs. I think of dogs as boys, because they stick around. When you have a dog, you've always got a pal. They don't get tired of you one day and go off somewhere else."

"Still," Charlie insisted, "it would be nice to keep her."

"Yeah, well . . ." Brad hadn't meant to argue against the idea. He'd been wanting a pet for so long that he didn't much care what this creature was, cat, dog, or piranha. She would do just fine. And, besides, a cat would be easier to hide than a dog. For a while, anyway. Cats didn't chase cars and they didn't have to be kept on leashes and, most important of all, they made very little noise. Someone working in his office in the basement all day, someone with other things on his mind, probably wouldn't even notice that a cat was hanging around.

The shed would be a perfect place for her to stay,

and they would only need to put out a bit of food and fresh water . . . and begin to make friends with her. Even a cat needed a friend.

"Bradley!" The summons came abruptly, and Brad suddenly knew why it had come, too, though he had forgotten until this moment. It was his turn on dishes, and he had left the house without doing anything more than stacking them on the counter. Mom had said she would call right at six, and Brad hadn't wanted to be near the phone when it rang. Even more, he hadn't wanted Charlie near the phone.

"Coming!" he yelled back. "I'm coming." And giving the mottled cat a last, considering look, he headed for the house.

Could he count on Charlie to keep their visitor a secret? If Dad found out before they'd proven themselves, he would take her to the Humane Society, for sure. Especially if he thought she was sick. And everybody knew what happened to animals that were taken there. An ugly, skinny–fat cat wouldn't have a chance.

He would finish the dishes, then he'd take some food to Cat. Charlie had left most of his supper hamburger on his plate, even though Dad had done them on the grill the way he liked. Brad could crumble that up for her. After this, he would leave something on his own dinner plate, too. He could think of all kinds of things he wouldn't mind sharing. Maybe she would like peas . . . or even better, asparagus. Or did cats eat only the good stuff, like hamburger and chicken?

Dad stood on the patio, pushing one hand through his dark curls with an impatient gesture that prompted Brad to reach up to touch his own hair, so like his dad's.

"You went off without doing the dishes," Dad announced when Brad had drawn close. He had that tight, now-you'd-better-listen-because-this-is-important set to his mouth. It was the way he'd looked so much of the time lately. "And I've told you, Brad. We've got to haul together. If we don't, this family's going to come apart."

This family has already come apart. Haven't you noticed? Brad thought, but he said only, "I wasn't leaving them, Dad. I just went out back with Charlie for a bit."

His father's face softened. "It's nice of you to pay a little extra attention to your brother, son. He's really hurting these days." He laid a hand on Brad's shoulder, but though the hand was large and warm and, Brad knew, intended to be friendly, it felt oddly like a burden.

Brad stepped out from under his father's grip. "I wish she could see what she's done to him. It ought to be her listening to him cry every night."

Dad sighed. "I wish he'd just go over there for the weekend. Her apartment's less than five miles away, and she'd come get him in a minute. She'd come get both of you, for that matter. You're really hurting her, staying away like you are."

"No!" Brad shook his head violently. That was all Brad needed, to have his brother leave, too. Not that he wasn't a pest sometimes. "Charlie doesn't want to go over there. He told me he doesn't." And then he added, more gently, "He likes it here, Dad. With you. We both do."

His father nodded, but he didn't look exactly thrilled. You'd think he'd be glad that they both wanted to stay with him, but he merely looked tired. He said, "Well, get started on the dishes, then," and turned away to get himself a bottle of mineral water from the refrigerator.

Brad waited until his father had gone into the living room and turned on the television before getting out a couple of small plastic bowls, the kind used for storing leftovers. He scraped the ketchup off the remains of Charlie's hamburger — he had a feeling that cats didn't like ketchup — and crumbled the meat into one bowl. Then he poured the milk left in Charlie's glass into the other. Charlie had never been a big eater, but he'd practically been living on air for the last five days since Mom had gone. Brad glanced at the clock. Five days and nine hours and thirty-three minutes. Not that anybody was counting.

Brad turned to his work. If Mom had her way, they'd be spending every weekend shut up in her dinky apartment. And then in the fall, when school started again so it didn't matter that she'd be at work during the day, she expected them to spend every other week with her. *Shared custody,* it was called. But who wanted to be passed back and forth like borrowed books?

Mom had thought that just because her apartment had a pool about the size of a postage stamp, they'd like coming there. So what if all their friends would be miles away? So what if the apartment was so far from their school, they'd have to ride a bus? So what if they wouldn't even have a bedroom there but just a lumpy bed that pulled out of a couch, and a dresser stuck away in a closet? Mom looked real proud when she showed them the bed and the dresser, like they were supposed to be thrilled that she'd reserved all that space for them.

"Some day," she said in that wistful voice she used when you knew she was talking dreams, "I'll be able to get a bigger apartment. One with two bedrooms, so you boys will have a room of your own." *Room,* she said, not *rooms,* though they had each had their own bedroom since they were born. Not to mention a big yard. Not to mention a park with a lake and a swimming beach just a couple of blocks away. Who needed a puny swimming pool?

The day they'd visited the apartment, right after she moved in, she gave them each a snorkeling set.

The snorkels would have been kind of neat if the pool had been bigger. Or if there were something to look at in a pool. But there was nothing to do with them except swim in circles, like goldfish in a bowl. And then when it was time to go, she wouldn't let them take the snorkels home. She said they should leave them there to be used in the pool. Like they'd want to come back if the snorkels were there. Like she really thought they could be bribed.

Even Charlie couldn't be bought off that easily. At least he couldn't after Brad explained it all to him.

They had something a whole lot better than snorkels here, anyway. They had their dad, their house, their friends, their school, their lake. They had their lives. And, now, they even had their very own cat. The only thing missing here was a mother. Their mother.

Brad had just settled the last of the dishes into the dishwasher and was wiping off the counter — he hoped Dad noticed, but he probably wouldn't — when Charlie burst through the door. A scratch ran down one cheek, starting only a fraction of an inch from his left eye, but though he was yelling, it wasn't about the wound.

"Brad, Brad, you've gotta come! Cat is dying! I mean it! There's blood and everything!"

"Hey! Whoa! What are you talking about?" Brad

grabbed Charlie by both shoulders, bringing him to a halt in the middle of the kitchen floor.

But slowing him down didn't improve Charlie's message. "Her insides are coming out," he shouted. "I saw it. They're just squeezing right out!"

Brad glanced quickly in the direction of the living room to see if Dad had overheard. Fortunately, the volume was turned up on the TV. Their mother had hated that, Dad watching TV every evening and with the volume turned up, too. But right now Brad was relieved.

"She's not dying, Charlie," he said quietly, trying to sound more sure than he really was. The cat had looked bad, after all. Real bad, now that he thought about it. "Get hold of yourself." It was something Dad said when anyone got too upset. Brad picked up the bowl of crumbled hamburger and thrust it into Charlie's hands. "She's probably just hungry or something."

He picked up the bowl of milk himself, turning Charlie around with his free hand and moving him toward the door. Again, he glanced in the direction of the living room. If Cat really was sick, they might have to tell their father, but not until they clearly had no other choice.

Charlie was still blubbering, and Brad directed him out the patio door and toward the toolshed. "Tell me what happened, anyway," he demanded when they were away from the house.

Charlie took a wavering breath. "I was watching her, just sitting there in the doorway, watching, and she started to act kind of funny, you know?" He looked at Brad as though he expected him to know.

All Brad could see was the scratch that had come so close to Charlie's eye. What would his father have to say about "responsibility" if he, Brad, was hiding a stray cat that blinded his brother? "What did you do?" Brad demanded, not waiting for the rest of the story. "How'd you manage to get yourself scratched?"

Charlie ran one dirty finger the length of his cheek, but then he shrugged the scratch away. "I was just trying to help. And when I got up close, she went kind of wild."

"Well," Brad said, "we've got food for her now. That'll . . ." But he never had a chance to finish saying what the food would do for her, because they had arrived at the door of the shed. Brad took up the flashlight that Charlie had dropped in the grass and shone it into the corner.

"See," Charlie said, and Brad saw.

Cat was still there, lying in the straw, her eyes two points of reflected light. At least she was no longer rumbling with that too-loud, too-ragged purr. Instead, when the beam from the flashlight hit her, she let out a low growl, and Brad knew what to do about that. He stepped back. But not before he had seen.

Charlie was right. Cat was coming apart. Something had emerged from beneath her tail, a whitish-gray sack still attached to her body by a long string, and she was licking at it. Licking and growling and licking.

CHAPTER THREE

"She's dying, isn't she?" Charlie jostled against Brad, trying to peer past him. "You don't have to tell me. I know she is."

But though Brad knew it, too, he wasn't ready to say so. Saying things made them so...definite, somehow. He had been that way about Mom, too. Even after he'd known she was going to go, even after she'd *gone,* he hadn't wanted to talk about it. As though refusing to say the words could keep it from being true.

Now he replied, "Of course not. She's just..." But he couldn't finish the sentence, because he didn't have any idea what it was that she was *just* doing...except, of course, dying as Charlie had said.

Ignoring the continuing growl and the sound of Cat's rough tongue grating against the surface of whatever she was licking, he shone the flashlight more closely, still keeping a careful distance. The whitish membrane was starting to tear. Despite the dark taste that had climbed into his mouth, Brad stepped forward. With the membrane torn, he could begin to make out a tiny, pink-and-black shape.

"I told you. She's not dying!" he shouted, realizing suddenly what he was seeing. And then more softly when Cat flared her ears and raised the pitch of her growl, "She's having kittens!"

"Really?" Charlie leaned around him for a better look, but turned immediately away again. "I didn't know it was so gross . . . having kittens," he said, his voice going tight.

Brad didn't reply. Charlie was wrong, but there was no point in saying so. It wasn't gross. Not the least bit. In fact, it was the most exciting thing Brad had ever seen. The tiny creature was emerging from the silvery sac now, and he could see every part. The triangular nose. Delicate claws, curved and almost translucent. A stubby tail tapering to a point. Looking at the kitten, Brad felt a rush of gratitude, even of love, for Cat. What a wonderful thing she had done! What a fabulous creature she was to have brought this kitten, whole and alive, into the world!

Cat kept licking the baby, and in response to her vigorous washing, it took its first shuddering breath. Then another and another. As the fur dried under the mother's busy tongue, the parts that had seemed to be pink began to look white. It was a black-and-white kitten! And beautiful! Well, maybe not beautiful, exactly. Its eyes were sealed shut; its tiny, round ears were folded tightly against its skull; its head was too large for its body. But, still . . .

The mother went back to gnawing what Brad realized now was the umbilical cord. As soon as the kitten was freed, it bumped its blind way to her belly to suck. How astonishing it was that the kitten could be so tiny, so minuscule, really, and yet know exactly what to do.

The kitten had a black mask that covered both eyes and flowed down its back like a cape. Only the tip of its tail and its belly and legs were white. Three of its four paws were black, too.

"Have you ever seen anything like it?" Brad whispered. He had known about birth, of course. Years ago Mom had given them a book that told all about it. But reading words, seeing drawings, even photos, was nothing like this. How could he have known that everything about a new kitten would be so perfect, so complete? Why, there were even stubby black-and-white whiskers!

This was just about the most incredible thing that had ever happened to him. Not only was Cat not sick, not dying, but it was clear that she was going to stay. It was almost as if she had delivered this kitten to him.

"Isn't it great?" he said, prodding Charlie with his

elbow to elicit some kind of response. "Isn't it absolutely incredibly fantastic?"

"Yeah," Charlie agreed, but he sounded a bit faint.

"We've got to name him. Something special. He *is* really special, you know. You can see that. I think this one's even a boy. What about . . . what about . . ." Brad searched for the kind of name their mother might have come up with if she had been here. Something good enough to prove that he could do it without her help.

"I think she's going to have another," Charlie said, his voice going tight again.

Brad squatted in the straw to watch. The mother cat was straining, her eyes squeezed closed, her entire body rigid, and a translucent balloon was emerging from beneath her tail. It grew until it was the size of a marble, then half the size of a Ping-Pong ball. When Cat went limp again, the balloon disappeared back inside. Brad turned the flashlight on Charlie. He blinked in the harsh light and put on a grin, but his face had gone pale. His freckles stood out like dark stars against a whitish sky.

Brad turned the light back on Cat. She was lying still, apparently waiting for more to happen. The black-and-white kitten, oblivious to his mother's effort, was still nursing, pummeling her belly with one white and one black paw. Brad reached a cautious finger out and ran it the length of the kitten's back. The fur was still slightly damp, but soft. Very soft.

The mother cat gave a warning growl, and he pulled his hand back quickly.

Was this the way all babies were born? Was it always such hard work? How could any mother walk off and leave her children after she'd been through so much just getting them here?

In about ten more minutes, a second kitten had emerged. Not as beautiful as the first, but still another whole, new kitten. This one was mottled, exactly like the mother. Even its face was divided like hers, half light, half dark. Again Brad reached to run a finger down the black-and-white kitten's back — down *his* kitten's back — and whispered to Charlie, "I know. We can name him Tuxedo."

"Who?"

"The kitten, of course. The black-and-white kitten."

Charlie nodded solemnly. Brad could tell that he was impressed with the name. Probably impressed with how quickly Brad had thought of it, too. Mom always said she had to "sleep on it" before she could come up with anything good.

Brad settled back into the straw and took a deep breath. What could be more perfect than this? Tuxedo would be his, of course. Charlie could have the mottled kitten. And the mother . . . well, they could share her.

"Are we going to tell Dad now?" Charlie asked. "About the kittens, too?"

Brad considered that. Their father had been trying

hard these past few days. You could tell how hard he was trying by how carefully level he kept his voice. Even when Charlie had dropped the carton of orange juice in the middle of the kitchen floor yesterday, he hadn't yelled. He hadn't even sounded cross. He'd just sighed and said, "Okay, Charlie. Clean it up." And then he'd gone down to his office to work. He'd gone without having any breakfast himself, though, so you knew he was upset.

Dad didn't even complain about Charlie's crying at night, or say, "Get hold of yourself, son," the way he usually did. But you could tell that it was taking a lot of effort, controlling himself so much. Which made it seem like not exactly the best time to talk to him about keeping a cat. Three cats. Or maybe more. Who knew if the mother was done "coming apart" as Charlie had seen it?

"Are we going to tell him, Brad?"

Brad shook his head. "Not yet. We'll take care of them ourselves for a while. Just until Mom comes home. She'll let us keep them for sure."

"But what are we going to feed her? She takes care of the babies, but the mama's going to need food."

Brad looked down at the little family, smiling to himself. The second tiny kitten had made its way — her way, she must be a girl since she looked so like the mother — to her mother's belly and was nursing as eagerly as Tuxedo. Charlie was such a worrier!

"That's easy," he said. "We just bring her the leftovers from our plates like I did tonight."

"Won't Dad get mad?"

Their father was a stickler about wasting food, about wasting anything, really. It was something else he and Mom used to argue about. Dad's favorite meal was to take all the leftovers from the refrigerator and make what he called "soup." Mom called it "garbage soup" and after her and Dad's usual fight, she'd order pizza for herself and Brad and Charlie when she came home to find it bubbling on the stove. One time, just to prove something — Brad had never known what — Dad had made a huge pot of garbage soup and eaten it for an entire week, three meals a day. The rest of them had pizza and Chinese takeout and Big Macs and macaroni-and-cheese and even, one night, an entire supper of nothing but popcorn and hot cocoa. It had been a great week . . . except for the strained silence when Mom and Dad had been in the same room.

Still, Brad said, "He'll never notice. Not now, anyway. He's trying too hard."

"Yeah," Charlie agreed, clearly relieved. "You're right."

Mother and babies were resting nicely, and in fact, Cat had started purring again, a more even, softer purr this time, as she kept licking the babies, first one, then the other.

Charlie asked, "Is that all she's going to have?"

Brad sighed. Sometimes Charlie was such a little kid. He often asked him those kinds of questions, as though, just because Brad was older, he was supposed to have answers for everything. Instead of replying, he said, to make things clear, "Tuxedo is mine. You can have the other one."

Charlie didn't respond. When Brad finally looked over his shoulder at his brother, he saw that his eyes had gone all wet. Crud. It was like that was all the kid could do lately, cry.

"Look, Charlie," he said, explaining it all as reasonably as he could. "I'm the one who discovered him."

"And I was here when he first started to be born."

"But you didn't even know it was a kitten. You thought it was the mother's insides coming out. Remember? And, besides, I came up with a name for him, too."

Charlie didn't offer further argument, but now his chin was wobbling. Brad sighed again. He hated to see Charlie cry, but Tuxedo was his. He had to be! It was like he'd been sent especially for him.

"Just a minute," he said, on a sudden inspiration, and he jumped to his feet and went out of the shed, returning with a flat pebble. He held it out in front of Charlie and spat on one side.

"Okay," he said, "wet side I win. Dry side you lose. Fair and square. And if I get Tuxedo, then he's mine.

No arguments. No more tears. All right?" He talked fast, only half expecting to get the scam by Charlie. He was pretty sharp, for all his blubbering. But though Charlie gave him a considering look — and turned to examine the kittens again — he didn't seem to notice that there was anything wrong with Brad's no-win proposal, *wet side I win, dry side you lose*. He nodded, and Brad said, feeling suddenly generous, "Do you want to toss?"

Charlie took the stone, flipped it, and caught it again. Then he held his hand out.

"Wet side!" Brad called gaily. "I win. Tuxedo is mine!"

For a moment he was sure that Charlie was going to start bawling, or even worse, run to their dad. But he didn't. He just turned back to study the kittens again. "The little muddy one's prettier, anyway," he said, lifting his chin defiantly. "I'm glad she's mine."

"Yeah," Brad lied. "That one is real pretty."

He wished he felt better about winning the toss. In fact, now that he knew how it had come out, he wished he had just called *wet side* and taken his chances. He wasn't usually the kind of person who went around cheating little kids. Especially his own brother. But there were some things too important to risk losing.

"Here," he said, holding the bowl of crumbled hamburger out to Charlie. "Do you want to feed Cat?"

Charlie nodded and took the bowl. "Look, beautiful Mommy," he sang softly. "We've got something for you."

Brad smiled. The way he'd called the toss wasn't going to matter. Charlie would love the little mottled kitten, anyway, just because it was his. Maybe he would love it more because it was kind of ugly. Charlie was like that.

The important thing was that Brad had Tuxedo for his own.

CHAPTER
FOUR

"How did you get that scratch on your face?"

Startled, Brad looked up to see that Dad was staring across the supper table at Charlie. He had assumed they were home free on this one. It had been two days since Cat had scratched Charlie, and the wound was already beginning to heal. But Dad sat there, a bacon-lettuce-and-tomato sandwich clenched in his hands, examining Charlie as though he were seeing him for the first time.

Charlie's hand flew to his cheek. "Oh," he said, turning a guilty red. "This?"

"Yes," Dad said, his mouth twisting slightly. "That."

Brad wanted to leap in with an explanation before Charlie messed everything up, but his brain seemed to be spinning in neutral. He'd been so busy taking care of Cat, gathering food, making sure Dad wasn't watching when he headed back for the shed, that it hadn't even occurred to him to be ready with some kind of story about Charlie's face. Or about the multitude of scratches on his own hands and arms, for that matter. He set his sandwich down and lowered his hands to his lap. He should have realized this would happen. These days Dad seemed to alternate between not seeing them at all and worrying about everything he did notice.

Before Brad could come up with anything, Charlie blurted, "I got scratched by a cat." And, then, apparently realizing his mistake, he ducked his head, cast Brad a pleading look from beneath his eyebrows, and added, "I mean, sort of."

Brad couldn't believe it! What did Charlie think he was doing? There were a million ways the kid could have gotten scratched that had nothing to do with cats, and Brad could think of all of them now. He could have said he'd been in a fight with Geraldine. She lived down the street, and even Dad knew she was a bully. Or that he'd been climbing a tree. Or he could even have said he'd scratched himself with a clothes hanger when he was picking up his room. Their father couldn't have complained about that.

Dad reached across the corner of the table and tipped Charlie's face to the light. "What cat? Where?" he demanded to know. "And what do you mean . . . sort of? That scratch barely missed your eye. You could have been blinded, do you know that?" He said it accusingly, as if Charlie had invited the cat to scratch him.

"She didn't mean to hurt me," Charlie answered, defending the cat instead of himself.

This is it, Brad thought. And for an instant, he was almost relieved at Charlie's blunder. Perhaps there had been no point all along in hiding Cat and her babies. Even though the kittens still looked rather uncomfortably like blind little mice, Dad might like them. Besides, if he was wrong and Mom *didn't* come back, no matter how determinedly he and Charlie stayed away, they would have to tell Dad sooner or later.

One glance at his father's face, though, and Brad changed his mind. He did not look prepared to accept anything new, least of all a cat that had just tried to put out his son's eye.

"It's Scott's cat," Brad said, the words tumbling out of his mouth almost before they had formed in his brain. "That's where Charlie got scratched. Over at Scott's. Scott has this stray cat who's kind of adopted him. She just came walking into his yard one day and stayed to have kittens."

Charlie stared at Brad, his mouth dropped into a soft O. You'd think it was the most astonishing story he had ever heard. Brad gave him a kick under the table, just hard enough to make him close his mouth.

"Scott named her Cat," Brad continued, his volume increasing, as though louder would also be more convincing. "Just Cat. Isn't that dumb?" He worked up a rusty laugh, but no one joined him. "And we were there checking out her kittens the other day, all three of us." He emphasized the *three,* wanting his father to remember that this was Scott's cat they were talking about here. "And, Charlie — you know how he is — went and poked his face in too close. So the mother was just protecting her babies. That's all."

He followed his explanation with a silent warning — *Don't you dare say a word!* And Charlie, having apparently recovered from his earlier astonishment over Brad's story, crossed his eyes in response. It was, Brad knew, a just-in-case-Dad-noticed version of a much ruder gesture. Charlie might be unable to manage a good lie, but he wasn't any kind of angel.

Dad sighed, but his gaze on Charlie had softened, and when he spoke his tone was concerned. "Cats can carry diseases, you know." He reached across the table to pat Charlie's hand. "Especially strays that haven't had shots or any other kind of medical attention. That scratch could have made you sick . . . quite apart from the risk to your eye."

Brad said nothing, and to his relief, Charlie remained silent, too. They both waited for Dad to go back to eating his sandwich. Once he had, Brad waited for a couple more beats, then waggled his eyebrows at Charlie to indicate that apparently the danger was past. Charlie did not smile.

The rest of the week passed uneventfully. Dad disappeared, as usual, into his basement office or in front of the TV. Even when he sat across the table from them, he seemed to be concentrating on something he was watching inside his own head. Brad and Charlie overheard him once, talking to himself in the bathroom, carrying on a one-sided argument that must have been intended for their mother. "But why didn't you tell me?" was part of it. Along with, "Won't you give me another chance?" He sounded, Brad thought, like Charlie when he'd lost some kind of game.

A couple of times, when Brad had sat looking out of his bedroom window long after everyone else was asleep, he'd caught a glimpse of Mom's old beige Jetta cruising slowly along the street. He was pretty sure it was her car, anyway. Dad had picked it out for her years before, and she'd always referred to the color as "public-rest-room-paper-towel tan." If she'd had her choice, she probably would have had bright red . . . or now, perhaps, one of those colors that changed with the light.

Brad had rushed to the window and stared, but though the car had moved slowly through the puddles of deeper darkness cast by the trees, it had moved steadily, too, and he couldn't see whoever was inside. If it was her, she never stopped.

The only real problem Brad had that week was keeping Cat fed. The animal was voracious. At least she was voracious when the food in question was something she liked. When supper was BLTs, or cole-slaw and beans and corn on the cob or, even worse, garbage soup, she looked at Brad accusingly, like a teacher refusing an excuse for an overdue report, and turned back to her kittens. After a day or two of that, he'd taken to rummaging through the cupboard for food that would appeal to her. He'd found several cans of tuna, one of salmon, one of corned-beef hash. Tuna was Cat's clear favorite.

Brad rearranged the remaining cans each time he took something so that the shelves never looked empty, but Dad didn't seem to be noticing, anyway. If Brad hadn't gotten an advance on his allowance right after school was out so that he and Scott could go to Water World, he would have had money to buy real cat food.

But he *had* taken the advance, which meant that he wouldn't have any allowance coming for a couple more weeks. He couldn't ask for another advance, either. His father had lectured him for not having saved up for the outing, pointing out that he and Scott had been planning it since midwinter. When Dad had finally given Brad the money, he had made him promise not to ask for another advance for the rest of the summer. So there was no recourse there. And Charlie wasn't very good at saving money, either. Besides, at his age he didn't get enough allowance to buy much of anything, anyway.

The next Friday afternoon came, the day for *her* to call, and Brad kept Charlie close, making sure he didn't have a chance to turn traitor. Which was why Charlie was standing right there when Brad pulled the last can of tuna out from under his shirt, though he'd been careful to bring out the other "borrowed" cans when his brother wasn't around. There were some things Charlie was just too young to understand.

When Charlie saw the tuna, his mouth dropped open exactly the way it had in response to Brad's explanation at the table, only this time he burst out with, "Where'd you get that?"

"I bought it," Brad lied, taking his Swiss army knife out of his pocket and beginning to crank the can open.

"No, you didn't. You don't have any money." Charlie sounded, not just sure of himself, but decidedly smug.

"Okay, then, I took it from the kitchen cupboard. Cat is hungry."

Charlie stood with his feet apart, his hands on his hips. "That's stealing," he announced. He looked like a small version of a traffic cop.

"No, it's not." Brad felt like giving Charlie a quick punch, but he didn't. He had to keep his brother on his side. "The food in the kitchen belongs to all of us. It's not stealing when you take what's already yours." Charlie didn't look impressed, so he added, "Besides, do you want Cat to go hungry? You know she can't feed your kitten unless we're feeding her."

"You said we'd feed her leftovers, stuff from our plates."

"Yeah . . . well." Brad dumped the tuna into one of the plastic bowls and set it a couple of feet from the nest so Cat would have to move to get it. Feeding her away from the kittens gave him a chance to touch Tuxedo. "Cats don't like most of the stuff Dad fixes. They're carnivores, you know."

"What's that?"

"Meat-eaters, stupid."

"I'm not stupid." Charlie scowled, his face clenched like a fist. And then he added in the same aggrieved voice, "Still, it's stealing. You know it is. You're not supposed to take stuff from the kitchen without asking."

"That was Mom's rule, and Mom isn't here."

"It's Dad's rule, too."

Brad turned to study the kittens, ignoring Charlie. The kid was clearly trying to pick a fight, though Brad wasn't sure why. He didn't especially want to know, either. What he really wanted was to hold Tuxedo, but he didn't dare. He had picked up Tuxedo only once, and to his amazement the black-and-white kitten had lifted his trembling head on its spindly neck and hissed. Actually hissed, as though the ridiculous mite thought he was a whole, big cat! At the sound, Cat left her food and came at Brad with her head lowered and the fur rising along her spine, and he put Tuxedo down so fast that he almost dropped him. He'd been lucky, actually, to get out of there with all his skin.

What spirit Tuxedo had, though. What a great cat he was going to be! It would take time for him to know that Brad was his friend — the same way it was taking time for Cat — but that was all right. If he kept bringing food, they would both get used to him. Already, Cat didn't growl so much when he came close.

Charlie approached the kittens and squatted in front of the nest. "Mine has one eye open," he pointed out, clearly still trying to get some kind of a rise out of Brad. "And both of Tuxedo's are closed."

Brad grunted. Charlie was right. The mottled one did have one milky-blue eye open, and Tuxedo's were still shut tight. It wasn't fair, really. The dull girl kitten getting out ahead of Tuxedo like that. Probably by tomorrow morning, though, both of Tuxedo's eyes would have come open, and the mottled girl would still be peering at the world through one.

Brad ran a finger down Tuxedo's back. As much

as he had grown, that was still all it took to pet him, just one finger. Often when he stroked the tiny creature, Tuxedo lifted slightly, pushing against Brad's finger. But now the kitten was sleeping so soundly that he gave no response.

"I told you mine was better than yours," Charlie said in the same taunting voice. He was really pushing it. Ordinarily, Brad would have let him have it by now, and Charlie would have run to Mommy, bawling, and . . .

But he couldn't afford any of that today. If he got Charlie mad, he'd insist on answering the phone when Mom called. And he'd probably agree to go over there for the weekend, too. Which would spoil everything.

Besides, it didn't matter what Charlie's kitten did or when her eyes opened. Brad had the kitten *he* wanted.

"Better wake up, fella." He ran a finger again down the soft black fur of Tuxedo's back. "Dinner's being served." Cat had licked the bowl clean and settled into the straw with her babies. The three-colored kitten was already nursing vigorously, kneading her mother with tiny, mottled paws. Tuxedo hadn't stirred.

"See," Charlie said, "your kitten is so lazy, he won't even wake up to eat."

Ignoring Charlie was beginning to take real effort.

Brad ran the same finger down Cat's flank. To his amazement, though she lifted her head and looked at him sharply, she neither hissed nor growled. They were making progress. He would have commented on it to Charlie, but he knew his brother would just say something else crabby.

Which he did, anyway. "I'm gonna tell her," he said next. "I'm gonna tell her you've been stealing from the cupboard."

Her. It's what they called their mother, lately. Even Dad did it, refusing to say *Mom* or *your mother* or even *Jeanne*, the way he used to. Saying it was like calling her back. Calling her and having her refuse to come.

"Are you going to talk to her when she calls, then?" Brad turned to his brother, filled with defeat. It was so unfair. Charlie was going to ruin everything, and there was nothing he could do to stop him. "Don't you care if she never comes home?"

Instead of replying, Charlie picked up a long piece of straw, stuck it into his mouth, and chewed on the end so that it waggled up and down. He looked like some codger out of a movie about old times. He also looked like a little kid who was clearly enjoying his brother's discomfort. Brad doubled his fists, but made no move. Charlie was in charge here, and they both knew it.

"I didn't say that," Charlie said finally.

"Are you?" Brad persisted. "Are you going to answer the phone?" He leaned toward Charlie until they were practically nose to nose.

Charlie stared back at him, his eyes as pale and unblinking as the cat's.

"It'll spoil everything, you know. Everything." To Brad's own surprise, his voice caught in the middle of the sentence, half-hiccup, half-sob. He hadn't had the slightest warning that he was going to do that.

Charlie looked even more surprised than Brad was, surprised and embarrassed. He tossed away the straw he'd been chewing on, and scrambled to his feet. "I won't answer the phone," he said. "I promise." And without a backward glance, he turned and hurried out of the shed.

Brad leaned back in the straw and took a deep breath. Charlie would keep his word. He knew that. Why, then, why was he still so worried?

CHAPTER
FIVE

For a long time Brad sat watching the mottled kitten nurse. Tuxedo was still sleeping. It made Brad a bit uneasy, seeing his kitten lying there so still when he should have been part of the action, but then it hardly made sense to worry just because a kitten was asleep. He had seen a nature program on television once that had shown lions lying around dozing. The narrator had said that the big cats averaged sixty-seven naps a day. Apparently, sleeping was just what cats did, whatever their size.

All three of the cats were asleep when Brad left. Stopping in the doorway to stretch, he glanced at the sun and wondered what time it was. Was it almost time for *her* to call? He tried to shake off the slight uneasiness crawling up his spine. Where was Charlie?

Brad searched the yard and the house thoroughly without finding any sign. He didn't especially want to check with his father. Who knew what questions Dad might ask in return? But hoping, finally, that Charlie had asked permission to go over to one of his friend's, he stopped at the door of his father's office and said casually, "Hey, Dad. Have you seen Charlie by any chance?"

His father's head snapped up. "No." There was an edge of instant concern in his voice. "Isn't he with you? I haven't seen him for hours."

"He is . . . I mean he was . . . until just a few minutes ago." Brad put up a hand like a crossing guard halting traffic and backed away from the door. "Never mind. He's probably just in his room reading or something. I'll check there."

But Dad continued to sit with his head lifted as though he were sniffing the air for danger. He was like that, had always been like that. He worried about things . . . about *them*. Mom said he made mountains out of mole hills. Dad said terrible things could happen . . . and, of course, they could.

"Son," he asked, fixing Brad with a penetrating gaze, "is Charlie doing okay? Are you?"

It was such a direct question, and Dad's voice seemed so tired — and so very sad — that, once more, Brad teetered on the edge, ready to spill everything: Cat, the new kittens, his plan for getting Mom to come home, his struggle to keep Charlie from spoiling it all. But while he stood there, searching for a place to begin, his father's gaze wandered back to settle on the computer, and Brad turned away, answering roughly, "He's fine. We're both fine."

"Tell me if you don't find him right away," Dad said, already engrossed in the numbers, and Brad didn't bother to reply.

Charlie wasn't in his room, of course. Brad had looked there first thing. In fact, the kid had probably just tucked himself away in some remote corner of the house to sulk. But by the time Brad had checked all the places he could think of — and seen from the kitchen clock that it was almost five — he was beginning to wonder if his father hadn't been right to worry. It was clear that Charlie had gone off somewhere, but the question was *where*?

Charlie had agreed that he wouldn't answer the phone when Mom called, though it was clear that he wanted desperately to talk to her . . . and to be invited to come for the weekend, no doubt. He had promised, though, and he was a kid who kept his promises, even when they were inconvenient. Once, when Charlie was in the first grade, his teacher had made him promise to stop talking in class. A week later she was calling home, trying to figure out what was wrong. Charlie wouldn't speak, even when she called on him!

Thinking about the promise brought an idea crashing down on Brad with the force of a boulder. There was something Charlie *hadn't* promised. He'd said he wouldn't answer the phone when their mother called, but he hadn't said that he would stay away from her apartment. The two of them had been there only once, right after she had moved in, and she had driven them that time, so Brad wasn't sure Charlie knew how to find the place on his own. But he was certain, suddenly, absolutely certain, that Charlie had set out to go there.

For a moment Brad thought of going back into the house and telling Dad about his suspicions, but he knew exactly how that would go. If Dad found out that Charlie wanted to be at Mom's, he'd simply take him there. For the weekend, for however long Charlie chose.

"We trust you," Mom and Dad had said, as though this separation were some kind of game that would work out fine if only they played by the rules. "You're both old enough to decide for yourselves."

So Charlie was deciding. He was deciding to let Mom know it was all right for her to stay away. And Brad had to find him, to stop him.

He climbed onto his bike — Charlie hadn't taken his, so it wouldn't be hard to catch up with him — and set off in the direction of the apartment. Charlie was too little to go off on his own like that, anyway. The kid was lucky to have a big brother who cared enough to go searching for him.

For the ten-thousandth time, Brad wished that *she*

were around to see how much trouble she was causing. But, then, if anyone was going to cause trouble, it was always her.

Dad used to say so. He used to complain about lots of things, but especially because she couldn't stay within the budget he'd set up. Food, clothes, doctor bills — things like that she'd managed just fine. But she was always buying something that there wasn't even a category for in the budget. Like the time she'd come back from a vacation with a $250 piece of baleen. It had been part of a whale's mouth once, and it was eight feet long and hairy, and she'd brought it home and hung it on the wall. Dad grumbled under his breath every time he looked at it.

Or the time she bought Dad a Sherlock Holmes coat from a catalogue, though it wasn't even his birthday. It was incredibly ugly and incredibly wonderful, with big yellow-and-brown hound's-tooth checks and an attached shoulder cape. When Dad put it on, Mom laughed and laughed, and he did look rather like a duck in it. It was Dad who rewrapped the package and sent the coat back.

But the day after she took Brad and Charlie on a hot-air balloon ride, she and Dad had the biggest fight of all. That was, as far as Brad knew, anyway, the last one they ever had. After that, everything around home got strained and quiet and very polite, and Mom began making plans for moving to her own apartment. Like that was supposed to be a good

trade, a couple of hours in a hot-air balloon in ex-
change for an entire family.

"I know you boys can't understand," she had said.
"I don't expect you to, really. But it's something I've
got to do. I'm suffocating in this marriage."

She'd been right about one thing, anyway. They
didn't understand. Even Charlie, who thought his
mama had made the sun and the moon and hung
them in the sky, might be ready to forgive her, but
he would never understand.

"It's not you," she had told them. "It's got nothing
to do with you." But of course, it had everything to
do with them. How could she think it didn't?

And always, over and over again, she'd told them,
"I need something more." As though "something
more" were a one-bedroom apartment where you
could walk into the bathroom and hear neighbors
you'd never met flushing the toilet. As though "something more" were swimming back and forth in a
dinky pool, staring at the seams in the concrete and
listening to yourself breathe through a tube.

Brad had ridden halfway to the apartment — he
was almost ready to give up, deciding either that
he'd been wrong about where Charlie was headed,
or that the kid had gotten lost — when he finally
spotted him. Charlie was trucking along the sidewalk,
his fists clenched and his skinny arms pumping. His
shoulder blades jutted out sharply. Brad wasn't sure
why, but something about those jutting shoulder

blades reminded him of Cat the first evening she had shown up.

"Charlie." Brad pulled along side.

But though Charlie must have been tired — he had covered more than two miles already — he lifted his chin in that stubborn way he had and increased his pace. He didn't even glance in Brad's direction.

"You want a ride?" Brad slowed his pedaling so he could keep even, his front wheel wobbling. "You must be wiped out."

"I'm not." Charlie squared his narrow shoulders. "I can make it just fine."

"But don't you want me to take you?"

Charlie stopped abruptly. Brad put on the brakes and caught the bike.

"Take me where?" He studied Brad skeptically.

"Wherever you're going."

Charlie rolled his eyes. He turned and began walking again.

Brad caught up. "You're going to Mom's," he said. "I know you are. Even though you promised."

Charlie stopped once more. His blue eyes behind the heavy lashes looked soft, but his jaw was tight. "The only thing I promised," he said, "was not to answer the phone when she called."

"I know," Brad said. And of course Charlie was right.

They stood in the middle of the sidewalk for a moment, neither of them finding anything more to say, until Charlie finally asked, "Would you really take me?"

Brad wouldn't, of course. It would be like chopping off his own foot. But still he said, biding his time, "Yeah. If you're sure you've thought this through."

Charlie let out a huge breath. "I've thought it through and through. That's all I've done since she went away is think about it."

"And?" Brad asked.

"And," Charlie said simply, "I want to live with her. Part of the time, anyway. And I want you to come, too. It won't be so bad, Brad. Really."

It won't be so bad! Brad wanted to laugh except that it wasn't funny. Their lives ruined, all of their lives ruined, and here was Charlie saying, *It won't be so bad!*

Brad wanted to shout, to bring down the sky with his yelling, but that wouldn't help him get Charlie turned around. He spoke in a quietly controlled voice. "Do you realize what you're doing, Charlie? If you go over there, it'll spoil everything — she'll never come home." And when Charlie said nothing, he asked, "Which would you rather do, go live with Mom part of the time, or have her come home like we talked about?"

Charlie stared stubbornly at the sidewalk. "I'll bet she thinks we don't love her anymore. I'll bet she thinks we don't even *like* her!"

"But that's the point, Charlie. Don't you see?"

Charlie shook his head. Clearly he didn't want to see. "She said she wasn't coming back. She said she'd decided for sure."

Brad squeezed the handgrips on his bike until his knuckles ached. "I know what she told us. She said she'd made up her mind. She said there was no point in arguing, or begging, either. But that was because she thought we were going with her. Do you suppose she'd thought for a minute about what it would be like all alone, without us, in that crummy little apartment with the crummy little pool?"

"Yeah, well . . . " Charlie said.

Brad pushed on. "And if we don't answer the phone when she calls, and if we don't go over there, and if we don't use her silly snorkels in her silly pool, she'll get so bored and so sad and so lonesome, she'll come back home. She'll just have to! Then things will be perfect. We'll get to live at home and have Mom and Dad, too."

Charlie considered that carefully, his lower lip caught between his teeth. His two front teeth had come in longer than the rest, and they still looked outsized in comparison to the rest of his face. Finally he said, simply. "But what if she doesn't?"

"What if she's just sitting over there," Charlie persisted, "feeling like you said, and still, she's not coming back . . . just like she said she wouldn't?"

And that was when Brad remembered the thing

he hadn't told Charlie, hadn't told him because he hadn't properly figured, himself, what it meant. Until this very moment. He bent close.

"I can prove that it's working," he whispered, "that she's already thinking about coming back, in spite of everything she said."

Charlie's eyes opened wide.

"I've seen her." Brad was still whispering. "Sometimes at night, after you've gone to sleep, I've seen her driving down the street, right by our house. Looking. Wanting to come home."

"Really?" Charlie was breathless. "Did she stop?"

Brad shook his head. "No, but she goes by real slow. And she wants to. You can tell she wants to because of how slow she goes. It takes her a *long, long* time to drive down the street." He stretched the *long, long* to let Charlie know how slowly she moved, how long she looked. And then he straightened and spoke in a more ordinary voice, "Just give her another week, Charlie. Two at the most. She'll be back. She'll come back and stay."

"And then she'll think up a name for my kitten. Won't she?" Charlie was grinning.

Brad smiled, nodded, and went immediately serious again. "But if you can't hold out, Charlie..." He paused. "If you can't hold out, then everything will be lost, don't you see? Everything?"

"I can hold out," Charlie promised, but behind the eager smile, his eyes were still sad.

It made Brad angry with their mother all over again, the sadness in his brother's eyes. When she did finally give up and come home, he was going to have a thing or two to say to her.

"Climb on," he said, gently. "I'll take you back." And he put his hands under Charlie's arms and helped him jump up on the crossbar.

They rode home in a companionable silence, a tuft of Charlie's hair tickling beneath Brad's chin. Brad wondered if he should have told Charlie about seeing Mom drive by at night. He *thought* it had been her car, but of course, he couldn't be sure. The same way he couldn't be absolutely certain that refusing to answer the phone, refusing to visit her at her apartment, would really bring her home. But, still, he had to believe it himself or what hope was there?

There had been something so definite about her plans, and when he and Charlie had been there, she had actually seemed elated over her new apartment. Like a crummy little place of her own was really what she needed ... or one part of what she needed, anyway.

Still, it was the only way. Arguing, even begging, hadn't helped before she'd gone.

They were passing the SuperValu, and seeing the supermarket gave Brad an idea. Cat was going to need more food, and the cupboard was practically bare ... of things a cat would eat, anyway. "Hey, Charlie," he asked. "Do you have any money?"

"Lots," Charlie replied, laying a grimy hand over his pocket.

"Then let's buy some cat food. That way we won't have to take any more stuff from the cupboard."

Charlie turned over his money willingly enough, all forty-one cents that represented his "lots." It was just sufficient to buy a small can of Seafood Supper, and with that tucked into one of the oversized pockets of Brad's shorts, they headed for home again.

"I'm going to check on the kittens," Brad said as they pulled up in front of the garage.

"I know how Tux is going to look," Charlie informed him. He closed his eyes and smacked his lips in imitation of a blind, suckling kitten.

Brad laughed and dumped Charlie off the bike. "Anyway," he said, "do you want to come?"

But Charlie didn't answer. He was standing in the driveway, gazing toward the house with a longing so transparent that Brad could feel it in his own throat.

The telephone was ringing.

CHAPTER SIX

The jangling cry of the telephone stopped abruptly. Neither Brad nor Charlie spoke.

"I'll race you to the shed," Brad said after a beat or two of silence. And waiting only long enough to make sure Charlie was going to run with him, he took off.

His legs were longer than Charlie's, of course. And, besides, Charlie had to be tired from his long walk. Brad expected to keep it at an easy lope and still beat his little brother easily. So he wasn't prepared for the determined burst of speed Charlie put on, or for seeing him pull ahead. Brad still got to the shed first, but he had to work at it, and that, too, was a surprise.

They both stopped in front of the open shed door,

doubled over, gasping. Brad waited for Charlie to straighten before he pulled himself upright, too.

"You're getting fast, Charlie. You about left me in the dust."

He could see the bright pleasure flash in Charlie's face and smiled at it. Charlie wasn't a bad little kid, actually. Not bad, at all. He needed someone to pay more attention to him, that was all. From now on the two of them had to stick together.

Brad stepped into the shed. He took the flashlight from the shelf and shone it into the corner. Cat stared back at him, unblinking, the way she always did. Her eyes were pale fires in the gloom of the shed.

"My kitten's still nursing." Charlie prodded him from behind.

"Yeah, yeah. She's a greedy little pig," Brad teased. He shone the light lower to reveal the kittens. As Charlie had said, the mottled kitten was still plugged in to the mother . . . or perhaps she was plugged in again. They hadn't been away for much more than an hour, so, of course, nothing had changed. Tuxedo was —

The light wavered in Brad's hand. He dropped onto his knees in the straw and, holding the flashlight against his chest to steady it, shone it more closely on the nest.

Tuxedo was sprawled exactly where he had been before, along his mother's side. Tuxedo was limp, flat, like a discarded scrap of fur.

Tuxedo was dead.

Brad didn't have to touch the black-and-white kitten or check for breath or heartbeat to know for sure, because the tiny creature had been torn open. His fur was chewed through, and the whorls of his tiny gut exposed. The mother cat gazed up at the two boys, her eyes innocent and round, and licked her whiskers.

She was purring.

Brad sprang to his feet, staggering backwards. "Did you see?" he cried. "Did you see?"

But it was obvious that Charlie had seen, because he had bolted outside.

Brad stumbled toward Cat again, meaning to grab her, to throw her, to hurl her out of the shed. A growl, deep in her throat, stopped him.

He wasn't going to leave her here, though. The murderer! The cannibal! She wasn't going to lie there in *his* straw, in *his* shed, growing fat on *his* food after killing her own kitten. Not only hers, either. *His!* Brad looked around for something to use to drive her away and, not finding anything, dashed out of the shed.

Charlie was leaning against the wall, crying. His kitten was fine, but still, there he was, blubbering all over himself. Didn't he know there wasn't any time for that? They had to *do* something.

A glance toward the corner of the house where the garden hose lay coiled gave Brad an idea. "Open the cat food," he ordered his brother, tossing him the can and his Swiss army knife to use on it. And he headed for the hose.

Brad turned the hose up full, then cut it off at the nozzle before dragging it back to the shed. Charlie was waiting, the can of cat food open.

It was one of the great things about Charlie. When you needed him for something important, he was there.

"Get Cat to come out of there," Brad ordered. "Use the food to make her want to come."

Charlie nodded and stepped to the door of the shed. "Here, kitty, kitty, kitty." His voice was high and innocent. "I've got something nice for you. Come on, kitty."

Brad held his breath, but there wasn't a sound from the shed, not even a rustling in the straw. Maybe between the tuna he had fed her earlier and the feast Cat had made of her own kitten, she wasn't interested in Seafood Supper.

"Hold the can lower," he commanded, "so she can smell it for sure."

Charlie obeyed, squatting to hold the open can almost at floor level, but keeping his neck craned so he was looking away. Clearly he didn't want to see the dead kitten again, and Brad certainly understood that.

Brad waited, cursing under his breath. What a

beast she was! As if they hadn't been feeding her ...
every day, many times a day. As if they hadn't been
doing everything for her.

"Here, kitty," Charlie called again. The hand holding the can shook, and he steadied it by supporting
his wrist with the other hand. "Come on, Cat." .

Brad stood waiting. The cold water seeping from
behind the nozzle trickled down his arm and
dripped off at the elbow, but he did nothing to re-
adjust his grip. His kitten was dead. What difference
did comfort make?

"Mew?" Cat said from the depths of the shed. It
seemed to be a question.

"Come on, Cat," Charlie called softly. "I've got
supper for you."

A moment later, Charlie stepped away from the
shed, and Cat appeared in the doorway. She kept
looking back over her shoulder toward the nest.
Seeing her pretend to be concerned about her babies that way sent heat flaring along Brad's skin, and
he squeezed the dripping nozzle, waiting for his
chance.

Finally, by moving slowly, Charlie managed to
draw the mother cat through the doorway and
around the side of the shed. Then he set the can
down directly in line with Brad and the hose and
stepped back.

Brad waited until Cat had dipped her nose into

the can. Then, standing only two feet from her, he twisted the nozzle so that a shining burst of water leapt from the hose and hit her broadside.

The blast tumbled her over, rolling her onto her back as effectively as a kick. Almost as fast as she had gone down, though, she was on her feet again, yowling. She bolted away, leaping for the tall, wooden fence that enclosed the neighbors' yard and making it over as easily as if there had been a ladder to climb.

She must have had enough momentum to scale the fence on the other side of the yard, too, because her piercing wail faded quickly into the distance.

Charlie jumped up and down, applauding, as though Brad had just performed some kind of magic trick. "You got her!" he yelled. Brad hadn't seen him so exuberant in weeks. "You ran that stupid cat off."

"Yeah, I got her," Brad agreed. Why didn't he feel better about seeing her run like that?

Charlie grabbed the hose and began twirling in crazy circles, holding it aloft so that the spray rained down on both of them. "That stupid, old cat!" he yelled. "That stupid, old, crazy cat. That crazy, nasty, mean cat!"

Brad watched, limp and exhausted, unable to join or even to appreciate the victory dance. It wasn't that

he felt bad for Cat. She deserved what she got...
and more. Much more. But there was something
about the sound of her wail — something almost human — that hung in the air still and filled him with
horror.

It wasn't until his brother stopped spinning and
stood staring at him, eyes wide with astonishment,
that Brad knew.

He was the one. The sound was coming from
him.

He was bawling.

Brad tamped the dirt down beneath the rosebush
and stood slowly, dusting his hands on his jeans.
That was the end of it. He wasn't going to cry anymore. Tuxedo was buried.

"Is that all?" Charlie scrubbed at his eyes with the
heels of his hands, creating a racoonlike mask of
mud. "Aren't you going to say a prayer or something?"

"Tuxedo doesn't need any prayers. He was a good
little kitten. If anybody needs prayers, it's his
mother."

"Well, she's not getting any from me."

Brad nodded grimly. She wasn't getting any from
him, either. He went to the garage to put the shovel
away.

When he returned to the backyard, Charlie was

standing in the doorway of the shed, peering into the corner where his kitten lay. She seemed to be sleeping as peacefully as if her mother and brother were still at her side. Charlie, however, looked totally miserable.

"She didn't hurt your kitty," Brad reminded him, laying a hand on his shoulder. But he couldn't help adding, internally, *it's mine who's dead*. It had obviously been a bad idea, cheating on the toss to get Tuxedo. But then who could have expected a mother to kill her own baby, and the best of the litter, too?

"My kitty's an orphan now," Charlie replied, his face beginning to crumple all over again.

"No, she's not." Brad rubbed Charlie's back. Beneath his moving hand, the ribs felt fragile and, somehow, vulnerable. "Her mother's just gone away, that's all. Besides, she's still got *you*. You can take care of her."

"I can't," Charlie wailed. "I don't know how."

Brad kept rubbing. "Don't worry. I'll help. It's going to be okay." But even as he spoke, a knot pulled tight in his stomach. Would they really be able to take care of so young a kitten?

Once he and Scott had found a mother rabbit dead in the road, a nest of babies nearby. Their eyes were just beginning to open like Charlie's kitten's. So they had brought the babies to Scott's house, nestled them in a box, and fed them warm milk from a doll bottle they had borrowed from Scott's sister. In fact, they had labored for days over the little rabbits, trying everything they knew and everything Scott's mother could suggest, too. But still the bunnies had died, one after the other. It had made for the worst week of his life. The worst week until now, anyway.

The least they could do for Charlie's kitten would be to try, though, both try to feed her and try to keep the poor little thing safe. That meant they had to keep the shed door tightly closed so Cat couldn't return for another meal. You had to face it. There were some young ones who were better off without a mother.

Brad and Charlie got a saucer of milk from the kitchen and brought it to the shed. But of course, the kitten didn't know how to lap from a saucer. All she did, when they held her to the milk, was snort it, sneeze white bubbles, and then begin a high, piercing mew. It was amazing that so much sound could come out of so small an opening.

Finally Brad went to the house and returned with an old washcloth. He dipped a corner into the milk and poked it gently into the kitten's mouth. After a brief struggle, she set to sucking. But even so, she seemed to tire quickly, and by the third or fourth time they dipped the cloth, she cried, turning her head and refusing the offering.

Charlie held the wailing kitten against his cheek. "Maybe we should tell Dad," he said. "Maybe he'd know what to do."

"He'd know how to take her to the Humane Society if that's what you want!" Brad stood and brushed straw off his jeans. Why was he trying so hard to help, anyway?

Charlie didn't reply. He concentrated on tucking the kitten back into her straw nest. She was still mewing.

"Go ahead and tell him, Charlie. It's your kitten. But you'll never see her again if you do. If we can take care of her, though, just until Mom comes back . . ." He left the sentence dangling.

Charlie kept stroking the kitten. When he looked up finally, Brad knew he had won.

Brad held out a hand to help his brother to his feet. "You don't need to worry," he promised. "We'll find a way."

Charlie nodded, clearly reassured, and Brad tried to feel reassured, too.

It was up to him, all of it. And yet he knew no more about kittens than he and Scott had known about baby rabbits . . . except that they needed a mother. A *good* mother.

"I've got an idea," he said, drawing himself up to stand straighter. "First thing in the morning, we can go to the library. They'll have books about cats. I bet they'll even have stuff in them about how to take care of baby kittens."

"That's it," Charlie agreed, beaming as though

Brad had just solved every problem they could possibly encounter. "We'll go to the library."

Brad's stomach growled. It was nearly bedtime, and they hadn't had supper yet. Earlier their father had told them to fix their own whenever they were ready. Apparently he hadn't wanted to be around when their mother called, either. Brad said, "Let's go heat up some SpaghettiOs or something."

Charlie beamed his appreciation for SpaghettiOs, and together they stepped out of the shed. The dusky yard had the expectant hush of a church . . . until a mottled streak erupted, almost from beneath their feet, tore across the yard, and disappeared through the bushes in the back.

Brad caught his breath. Cat had returned! She had come for Charlie's kitten! And for the Seafood Supper, as well. The can sat on the ground in front of them, licked clean.

Brad slammed the door shut behind him and gave the empty can a kick. "She came back," he said. "Already, the murderer had the gall to come back."

A small moan escaped Charlie's lips, and he looked at Brad in that pleading way he'd taken on lately. As though, despite everything, he still expected Brad to make things right.

Brad put an arm across his brother's shoulders and gave him a squeeze. "If I ever get my hands on that cat again," he promised, "I'll kill her." And when Charlie's expression didn't waver, he added, more loudly still, "I'll kill her and skin her and hang her guts up to dry!"

"Yeah," Charlie agreed, nodding fiercely, though his voice came out thin. "Yeah! We'll kill that cat!"

From inside the shed, the kitten wailed.

CHAPTER
SEVEN

Brad leaned his chin on his hand and stared at the picture of the mottled cat in the book. He was so tired. He'd been up at dawn — without Charlie's help — to try to feed the kitten again, not with much more success than the first time. And he hadn't slept well, either. All night long he'd dreamed that Cat had come back, only this time she was after *him*!

The picture looked just like Cat ... and like Charlie's kitten, of course. Tortoiseshell, the color was called. Somehow the splotchy color seemed prettier when you gave it a name.

He turned the page and glanced across the table at Charlie. A lot of help he was turning out to be! Here they had come to the library first thing in the morning the way they had agreed, and he was sitting there reading an old copy of *Boys' Life*.

"Hey, Brad," Charlie said, "there's this really neat story in here. It's called 'The String Game.' This kid — "

Brad interrupted. "We came here to look up stuff about cats. Remember?"

"Yeah. Well, you've got the book. Have you found anything yet?"

"Not yet." He hadn't found information about taking care of an abandoned kitten, anyway. Besides learning the name tortoiseshell, however, he had discovered that all tortoiseshell cats, all three-color cats, for that matter, were female. The exceptions were so rare that they barely counted. So Charlie's kitten was a girl, as they had thought. But Brad didn't bother to explain any of that. Let Charlie look it up himself instead of sitting there reading stupid stories.

He turned a few more pages and came across a picture of someone holding a kitten, its eyes still closed, and feeding it from a medicine dropper. The heading said, *Care of Orphaned Kittens*. Exactly what they needed!

"Here it is!" he shouted. The woman at the table next to them gave him a disapproving glance, and he lowered his voice. "Come see, Charlie. I've found what we need."

Charlie dropped his magazine and scurried around the table to look. "What's that they're feeding her with?" he asked after he had examined the picture.

"It's a medicine dropper. Can't you see?"

Charlie frowned. "Where will we get one of those?"

Brad wished Charlie wouldn't turn everything into a problem. "Maybe we have one at home in the bathroom cabinet," he said impatiently, scanning the print for more information. "It says the best milk to use is something called KMR, Kitten Milk Replacer, 'available at your vet's.'"

Charlie looked even more concerned. "Won't that be expensive? Almost like buying medicine?"

"But, see," Brad pointed to the place on the page, "it says that you can also use evaporated milk."

Charlie bent over the book, his breath hot in Brad's ear. "What's that?"

"I think it's canned milk, you know? Like you buy in the grocery store. *That's* not so expensive. And there might even be some at home, too. I think Mom used to use it for cooking sometimes."

Charlie went back to reading over Brad's shoulder. "It says you have to keep the kitten warm. . . ."

"That won't be hard," Brad pointed out, his excitement growing. He was getting into this business of rescuing the kitten. Not for himself, of course, but for Charlie. "Even the nights are pretty hot lately.

And she kind of buries herself in the straw, anyway."

"And you have to feed her every three hours," Charlie said, still reading.

"Every three hours! Even at night?" Brad pushed Charlie aside to check. "Oh, it says after the kitten is three days old — and yours is more than a week now — you can skip one of the night feedings. That means the last one would be about midnight, and then you'd have to feed it again at six in the morning."

Charlie straightened up slowly. "You mean we have to go out to the shed at midnight?"

Brad grimaced. Their backyard *was* large. And dark at night. And there were no lights that they could turn on without alerting their father. Inside the shed it would be even darker. "Can you think of any other way?" he asked, half hoping Charlie might really come up with something.

"We could keep her in my room."

"As loud as she yells? Dad would hear her in a minute."

Charlie looked so crestfallen that Brad pushed aside the thought of the dark yard, of midnight and six A.M. feedings. "It's going to be all right. We're in this together, you know, and we'll pull your kitten through."

But Charlie was reading again. "Ooooh," he exclaimed. "Yuck."

"What now?" Brad looked at the place where Charlie was pointing, and he didn't have to read more than a couple of sentences before he wanted to yell *Yuck!*, too.

The book said it wasn't enough just to feed the kitten and keep it warm. You had to take care of the other end, too. Tiny kittens couldn't eliminate the food they had taken in without help. The mother cat licked them to stimulate their evacuation. That's what the book called it, *evacuation*. But it was really . . . Brad suppressed a giggle.

A human taking care of a very young kitten could get the same effect, the book explained, by rubbing gently beneath the tail with a soft cloth. Great. Just what he needed. It was going to be worse than changing diapers.

"It says here," Charlie pointed out, "if you don't take care of that end, too, the kitten will die."

"Yeah, well . . ." Brad took a breath. "Then we'll just do it, won't we?"

"I suppose so." But Charlie didn't sound exactly enthusiastic.

Brad looked at him sharply. "Remember," he warned, "this is *your* kitten. I'm not going to do all the hard stuff."

"I know." Charlie ducked his head.

Brad glanced at the rest of the article. They seemed to have everything they needed to know for now. Later, they could come back and look at the book again if they had questions. He wasn't going to risk giving all their plans away by walking into the house with a book about cats. Once Mom had come back and she'd gotten Dad to agree that Charlie could keep the kitten . . . well, everything would be different then.

Brad closed the book and signaled Charlie that it was time to go. "Aren't you ever going to name your kitten?" he asked as they started toward the door.

"I know" — Charlie grinned — "since you're helping me, I'll name it Bradley the Second. How about that?"

Brad groaned. "Don't do me any favors, okay?"

"Okay." Charlie shrugged. But after they had pushed through the heavy library doors into the staring sun, he added, softly, "Mom would have thought up a good name by now."

Brad winced. He wished Charlie wouldn't keep doing that. Talking about her just made waiting even harder. But he said only, "Let's go home and find some canned milk and the medicine dropper. And the soft cloth," he thought to add.

"Yuck!" Charlie said again.

Brad and Charlie stood in front of the kitchen cupboard. There was no canned milk. Absolutely none. They had gone through every shelf. There hadn't been any kind of dropper in the medicine cabinet, either.

"But we have to have it!" Charlie wailed.

"I know. I know." Already knowing the answer, he asked, "Do you have any more money?"

Charlie shook his head.

"You could tell Dad you need an advance on your allowance," Brad proposed, though he knew the answer to that one, too.

Charlie shook his head even more emphatically. "No way. He always gets mad when *you* do that."

"Not mad, really. He just lectures me. I figure I'm kind of doing him a favor, though, because it gives him a chance to talk about the big R. You can tell he likes that, even if he acts kind of mad."

"The big R?"

"Responsibility," Brad intoned in his deepest, most mock-serious voice.

"Oh." Charlie nodded with recognition. Then they both went back to staring at the depleted shelves. It was pretty amazing that their father hadn't noticed anything missing before now. Brad hadn't realized he had taken so much to keep Cat fed. If Dad ever came out of his office in the basement and started seeing things again, they were going to be in big trouble.

There was only one solution, and the thought sent an electric current buzzing along Brad's spine. He rotated his shoulders, trying to get rid of the buzzing, but the idea that had set off the current was still strong.

Their father's dresser. Every night their father emptied the coins in his pocket onto a tray on his dresser . . . and didn't pick them up in the morning.

They were going to be in trouble, anyway, or *he* was certainly, so why stop now? After all, a starving kitten was counting on them. He might as well make the trouble worthwhile.

"I've thought of something, Charlie," he said, slowly.

"Yeah?" Charlie gazed at him in that familiar way, all open and expectant, as though he'd never for a moment doubted that Brad would take care of everything. That kind of look made Brad feel tired . . . and more than a little scared.

Brad took a deep breath. "I've figured out a way to get the right kind of milk for your kitten. And a dropper, too."

Charlie's upturned face shone. "How?"

Looking into the innocent blue of his brother's eyes, Brad knew, suddenly, that he couldn't tell him what he had in mind. If Charlie got upset about taking food from the cupboard, how would he feel about stealing from Dad? "Never mind," he said. "You don't need to know how. But I can do it."

Brad had expected Charlie to pester him, to insist on knowing not only what he was going to do, but all the details about how he would do it. He was surprised — relieved and disappointed in equal measure — when Charlie just nodded and turned away. "Okay," he said. "You get the milk, and I'll go check on Bradley the Second."

"Don't call her that!" Brad said, more sharply than he had intended. And then he added, "Besides, didn't I tell you? Your kitten is for sure a girl. She has three colors, and the book said three-color cats are female."

Charlie paused to consider that for a moment, then offered with a lopsided grin, "Maybe I'll call her Jeanne."

Was Charlie serious? Brad couldn't tell. "That's not going to fit," he said a bit stiffly. "When Mom comes back, we'd have two Jeannes."

"Then I guess I'll have to wait for her to name the kitten," he replied with a shrug, and he pushed out the back door.

Brad looked after him, annoyed at the easy way Charlie had walked out, leaving him to produce the evaporated milk and the medicine dropper. But it didn't really matter how angry he felt at Charlie. They had a kitten who needed feeding.

He checked at the top of the basement stairs — Dad was still down there in his office; Brad could hear the computer keys clacking — and then moved swiftly up the other set of stairs to his parents' bedroom. His father's bedroom now.

He walked right up to the dresser. There was quite a pile of change in the tray. Mom used to pick it up in the morning and use it for meters and things since she worked downtown. But Mom wasn't here to pick it up.

How much would canned milk cost? And a medicine dropper? If he took all the money, Dad would be sure to notice. But if he went to the store without enough, he would have to come back to get more. Then they would lose more time. It had been a long time since the kitten had had a proper feeding, and the book said she needed to be fed every three hours.

His fingers trembling, but moving almost mechanically as if being controlled by somebody else, Brad began to pluck money from the tray. Six quarters, a nickel, three dimes. Half a dozen pennies, too. No. He put the pennies back. It was too noticeable that there were coins missing with so many gone. He dropped the money into his pocket and hurried out of his father's room, down the hall, and out the front door. In another fifteen or twenty minutes, he would be back with the right kind of milk for Charlie's kitten and a medicine dropper to feed her with.

With the right kind of milk, the kitten would soon be strong. Both eyes would open, her ears would prick, she would hold her tail high. And when they brought Mom and Dad out to the shed, she would prance through the straw toward them, mewing and purring, looking cute. They would have to see what a good job he and Charlie had done, how responsible they had been.

Which meant, of course, that they would have to agree, both of them, that the kitten could stay.

CHAPTER EIGHT

The plan worked perfectly! The coins Brad had taken were exactly the right amount to buy the dropper and a small can of evaporated milk. Actually, he had wanted a big can, but the small one would do for now.

The book had said it was important to sterilize the dropper, and they had done that. They had diluted the evaporated milk, too, three parts milk, one part boiled water according to the book's instructions. And they had fed the kitten every three hours, day and night, except for the three A.M. feeding, which the instructions had said they could skip. The rich milk slid into the kitten's mouth and down her throat. Brad had even used an old washcloth on her other end, though he'd found himself on his own when it came time for that. Charlie had announced that he would watch, "Just until I see how you do it." And after several days, he was still watching. Brad didn't mind, though. It made him feel good, both powerful and kind, to be the source of all the kitten's needs.

Charlie never once asked how Brad had gotten the milk and the dropper. He just accepted everything and rejoiced at the way his kitten thrived. He even took responsibility for tucking the remaining milk into the deepest corner of the refrigerator, where their father wouldn't come across it, but Charlie didn't seem surprised or ask any questions when the first can ran out and another appeared. Or when another appeared after that.

Nor did he raise questions when Brad came home with a few little cat toys along with the third can of milk. "For when she's bigger" was the only explanation he gave. "She doesn't have any brothers or sisters to play with, so she's going to need lots of toys."

The second time Brad went into their father's bedroom for coins seemed, if not easier than the first, at least less strange. This time he knew exactly how much was needed for a small can of milk and took only that. But still, his fingers trembled; the electricity buzzed along his spine, and as he'd found himself doing before, he spent the rest of the day watching his father and waiting for the ax to fall. Every time Dad looked in his direction, he shriveled inside.

The ax never fell, however, and when Charlie managed to spill the second can of milk before they had used even half, Brad returned to the dresser top in their father's bedroom again. His fingers were almost steady this time as he plucked the coins . . . and kept plucking until he had enough for a large can of milk and some for the cat toys he'd been looking at in the store. Apparently Dad had no idea how much money he dumped on the dresser most evenings. And since he was used to having it disappear into Mom's purse, he didn't seem to notice that it wasn't building up. But, then, there was a lot Dad didn't seem to notice these days.

Charlie had quit crying at night, and Dad didn't say a word about that. Nor did he comment on the fact that the boys were spending so much more time around home and so little with their friends. Or that Brad and Charlie were both drooping at the breakfast table, their eyes heavy with fatigue. *She* would have noticed all those things. Their father, the light sleeper, was apparently even oblivious to their slipping out every night at midnight and again at six A.M.

It was almost, Brad thought to himself, as if he didn't much care what they were doing.

And if his dad didn't care, Brad figured there was no reason for him to care, either. About the fact that they were hiding the kitten. About the food he had taken earlier. About the money. About anything, really.

The only thing Brad cared about was the kitten,

keeping her fed and keeping her safe from her marauding mother. They kept the shed door tightly closed, so she couldn't return to hurt the kitten. But as far as either of them could tell, she had vanished.

Once or twice, when it was time for a feeding, they found the kitten's tummy still round and full, and she turned away from the dropper of milk. If they tried to force it into her mouth, she let it dribble down her fuzzy chin. When that happened, Brad told Charlie that they must have fed her a bit too much the time before, that she just wasn't hungry yet. It was the only explanation that made any sense.

Brad didn't dare set an alarm for the late feeding lest the sound of it awaken their father, and waiting in his dark room for midnight to come, he often sat by his window, watching the street. He never saw his mother's car again, though.

Sometimes, sitting there in the dark, Brad had to remind himself that he was not a thief, not a liar and a cheat. Hadn't he done only what was necessary? And what better cause could there be than giving life to a helpless creature?

Cheating on the toss was the only thing he had done for himself, and he had certainly been punished more than sufficiently for that. The kitten he had "won" was dead. Everything else, all the risks he had taken, had been for Charlie's kitten, not even his own.

But now Brad was responsible for Charlie's baby.

He had to take care of her, by whatever means necessary. The tiny creature, who had both eyes open now and whose ears were beginning to prick, even mewed when he came into the shed. Mewed to say that she trusted him. Mewed to tell him that she counted on him to feed her, to keep her safe and warm, to keep her alive.

If they had told Dad, he would have turned Charlie's kitten over to the Humane Society. They tried to save animals there. Brad knew that. But they had so many. Who would have the time to feed a tiny kitten with a medicine dropper seven times a day . . . or the stomach and the patience to rub beneath her tail after every feeding? At the Humane Society, they "put down" the animals no one wanted. And "put down" was just a fancy way of saying that the animals were killed.

The days passed, and the kitten thrived. Brad figured that every day Mom stayed away was good. Even she would probably like the nameless kitten better when it began to be cute. From the pictures in the book, he figured that meant she needed to be at least three weeks old. Surely, if they kept up their campaign, Mom would be ready to come back by then.

In fact, everything was going so smoothly, so completely according to plan, that Brad was stunned when, one night at supper, Charlie looked at Dad across the table and said, "Remember that stray cat

Brad told you about? The one that had kittens over at Scott's?"

Brad choked on a mouthful of spaghetti and glared at his brother. Was he going to give everything away? Didn't he care what happened to *his* kitten?

Dad looked up from his plate, the beginnings of a frown gathering between his eyebrows. "You mean the one who scratched you? Are you still going over there and risking getting your eyes put out?"

"Don't worry," Charlie said. "The mother cat isn't there any more. She ran off. But she left a kitten behind. We've been — I mean, Scott's been feeding it. But he needs to find it a home."

The frown had descended to Dad's mouth now.

"Could we take her?" Charlie continued blithely, as if Dad had been sitting there looking interested and pleased over all he'd said. "She wouldn't take up much room or eat a whole lot or make noise or any kind of mess or — "

When Charlie had begun, Brad had slumped in his seat, knowing what the answer would be. And it came fast. Dad didn't even wait for Charlie to finish his recital of all the things the kitten wouldn't do. He was already shaking his head. It was enough to make Brad want to leap up from the table and throttle his brother. But there was nothing he could do except aim a kick, which missed Charlie and hit the leg of his chair, leaving Brad's toe throbbing.

"No pets," Dad said firmly. "I've got enough responsibility these days, taking care of you boys. I don't need a cat to worry about, too."

Who told you to worry? Brad wanted to say, though, of course, he didn't.

"But you wouldn't have to — " Charlie started, and Dad interrupted again.

" — I know. You boys would say you'd be responsible, but I remember the time Brad starved those mice he'd brought home from school. Not to mention the guppies we gave you!"

Charlie pushed his plate away, his lower lip thrust out as though he had really expected a different answer. Brad was wild with frustration. Couldn't the little twerp even remember that they were waiting for Mom to come home? There was no excuse for anyone's being so dumb.

And Dad . . . with his lecture about mice and guppies, neither of which had been seen in this house for years. He never forgot anything that you needed him to forget, and he never noticed any of the important stuff, like the fact that one of his sons, at least, might be growing up.

"Besides," Dad said, apparently registering Charlie's disappointment and speaking more gently now, "when you boys go stay with your mother, I'd be left taking care of your cat. Pets aren't allowed in her apartment, you know."

Brad couldn't stand it any longer. Dad looked so

smug, so downright pleased with himself to have come up with such fine reasons for refusing. "How many times do we have to tell you" — he shoved heavily away from the table so that his chair screeched against the vinyl — "we aren't going. We're staying right here . . . with you. Even if you don't want us!"

Charlie sucked in his breath, and his eyes went large and round. Their father couldn't have looked more stunned — or more angry — if Brad had reached across the table and slapped him.

"Brad, that's unfair!" Dad's lips had gone pale. "You know I want you . . . and Charlie, too. Your mother and I both want you. We've told you that a hundred times. At least. You're the one who's making things so difficult around here. Refusing to answer the phone when your mother calls. Refusing to go over there. Making Charlie refuse, too. Don't think we — "

"He's not making me!" Charlie protested, his voice rising to an offended screech. "Brad can't *make* me do anything."

But Dad ignored him, glaring, still, at Brad.

Brad lurched to his feet. "Why are you defending her?" he bellowed. "She went off and left us. And it's your fault. You're the one she's running away from. Or haven't you noticed that, either?"

Brad's father had never hit him, not even a tap on the butt when he was a little kid. But still Brad knew with absolute certainty what the man would do now, what he would have to do. He would rise up out of his seat, his fist clenched, and flatten him. It was only what he deserved.

But his father didn't rise, and his fist didn't clench. Instead, to Brad's horror, his face crumpled the way Charlie's always did just before he began to bawl. It actually folded in on itself, beginning with the soft skin around his eyes and ending with his mouth.

Brad didn't wait to see if his father was really going to cry. He slammed out the back door.

"Bradley!" The voice was suddenly fierce, and there were no tears in it. "You come back here!"

But despite the authority in the command, Brad stomped the length of the yard, and his father didn't follow.

He slammed into the shed, banging the door so hard that Charlie's kitten lurched awake, quivering. He stopped himself, then, and knelt in the straw to scoop the kitten into his hand.

"Don't worry, baby," he crooned. "Don't be afraid. I'm here." And he was. Whatever Dad said, Brad would see that this kitten his father didn't want got everything she needed. Everything!

In fact, he'd been looking at a corduroy cat bed at the hardware store down the street, soft and warm-looking. The perfect bed for a kitten who didn't have a mother to take care of her. Or a father, either, if you thought about it. The kitten's father hadn't cared about her from the beginning.

The corduroy bed cost too much to buy out of the change on the dresser, but since Dad worked at home, he rarely kept his wallet with him. It stayed right there, tucked into the corner of his dresser drawer.

And he kept real money in his wallet. Dollar bills.

Why shouldn't Brad take them? It was for a good cause, and Dad would never notice, anyway.

CHAPTER NINE

"Here you are, little one." Brad picked up the kitten and tucked her into the corduroy bed. He was glad he had chosen blue. The kitten's tortoiseshell fur looked splashy and bold against the pale fabric.

The kitten lay still for a moment in the unfamiliar bed, her toothpick legs splayed in four different directions. Then she lifted her wobbly head and began to mew, loudly.

Brad had never known a creature who cried so much . . . except for Charlie, maybe. He'd bawled again the evening before. Maybe Brad had been too hard on him, telling him how stupid he had been to ask their father if he could have a kitten. Of course, Dad would say *no*. Why did he think they were keeping the kitten hidden until Mom came home, anyway? Charlie was really beginning to get on his nerves.

Dumb kid!

"What is that thing? Where'd you get it?"

Brad glanced over his shoulder. Charlie was propped in the shed doorway in that peculiarly boneless way he had taken on lately. It annoyed Brad, all over again, seeing his brother there, but still he kept his tone friendly enough when he replied, "It's a bed for your kitten. Isn't it neat?"

Charlie didn't answer. He just stood there, gazing at the cat bed as though it were a pile of trash. The kitten was still crying, lurching over the surface of the blue corduroy and clambering up the side. Brad picked her up and set her in the middle of the bed once more, but immediately, she headed out again.

"She doesn't like it," Charlie pointed out. "You can see she doesn't. She wants to be in the straw."

Brad suspected that Charlie was right. As tottery as the kitten still was, she had managed to scramble again to the bed's rim where she clung, mewing. If her needlelike claws hadn't been caught in the plush corduroy, she would have toppled out. He extracted her claws from the fabric and set her in the middle of the bed again. "She's not used to it yet. That's all," he said. "Give her time. She going to like it just fine."

"So where'd you get it?" Charlie demanded again.

Brad had a sudden vision of himself, opening Dad's drawer, lifting out the slim, brown wallet, fingering through the bills. *A ten? No, better take a twenty. Then there would be plenty left over for buy-*

ing more milk when they needed it, too. And the kitten would have to have solid food pretty soon. The bill slid, crisp and green, away from the others. It crackled when Brad had folded it to stuff into his pocket. And it was still crackling in his pocket when he had walked out of the house.

"What difference does it make to you?" he replied, glaring. "I didn't notice you worrying about where the *milk* was coming from."

At first Charlie glared back, but gradually he lost ground, and his gaze slipped downward. For a long moment, no one spoke . . . except for the kitten, who was still mewing and scrabbling to get out of the bed. When Brad finally picked up some of the straw from her former nest and pressed it around her, covering the pretty, blue fabric, she grew quiet at last.

Charlie didn't say anything, not even "I told you so," but he didn't go away, either. He remained standing behind Brad, balanced there on the sill the way the kitten had been on the edge of the bed, and sniffed loudly several times. Brad didn't bother to check him out. If he didn't actually see the tears, he could pretend the kid was merely savoring the musky smell of earthworms that hung in the air after the morning rain.

"She hasn't come back," Charlie said, finally. His tone was accusing. "You said she'd come back."

For a moment Brad thought Charlie was talking

about Cat, but one glance at his brother's face made him realize his mistake. Of course. Charlie was talking about their mother.

"I didn't say it would happen right away," he explained, as patiently as he could. "We just have to wait for her to change her mind."

"But doesn't she even miss us?"

Brad sighed. "Of course, she misses us. She's just miserable missing us. She's even been telling Dad how miserable she is with us not talking to her. That's the point."

"The point of what?" The tears were definitely coming now. "I don't want to make Mom miserable."

Brad couldn't see what was so wrong about making Mom feel a little bit bad. She'd certainly done a job on them. Still, he stood and immediately bent toward his brother so they could meet, eye to eye. "But we've got to, Charlie. Just for a little while longer. She has to miss us so much that she can't stand it another minute. It's the only way she'll ever come back."

Charlie's lower lip wobbled. His nose was running, and he didn't even bother to wipe it this time. "*I* can't stand it another minute right now," he said, his voice very small.

"But don't you see? We've about got her. You can't spoil everything now. She'll be coming home any day." As he spoke, Brad grasped his little brother by both shoulders. He meant to hug him. That was, at least, what he thought he was going to do. He meant to hug Charlie long and hard until he was through crying, until he was through needing Mom, at least for a little while. Until they were through needing her together, maybe.

But there was something about the feel of his brother's scrawny arms, gripped tight in his hands. Something about the dampness of his face, the perpetual dampness of it, and about the freckles spattered across his cheeks, so much like Mom's freckles. There was something, especially, about the way Charlie was looking up into Brad's eyes, waiting, expecting him to make everything right. And what if he couldn't make anything right at all? What if everything he'd done was wrong?

Before he knew it was what he was going to do, he found himself shaking Charlie . . . hard. The tawny head bobbled back and forth on the skinny neck. The mouth opened, but no sound came out. No sound at all.

"If you answer the phone tomorrow . . ." Brad forced the words between clenched teeth. "If you try to go over there again, I'll beat you to a bloody pulp. I swear I will."

"I" — the words came out in jerks as though from a broken record — "won't . . . Brad . . . I . . . promise . . . really."

When Brad released his hold, Charlie was off balance and almost pitched to the floor. Brad grabbed him again, supporting him until his legs bore his weight. The kid was trembling.

"I'm sorry, Charlie. I didn't mean ..."

But Charlie had pulled away, and he was already heading toward the house. His back was rigid, his head high, and his steps stiff, as though he were a marionette being jerked along by strings.

Was he going in to tell Dad?

No. If Mom had been there, he would have told her for sure. But he wouldn't risk going down to the basement office to tell Dad.

Would his little brother ever trust him, ever look to him for answers or comfort again?

That was another question entirely.

Brad stood over Charlie's bed, watching him sleep. It was time for the midnight feeding. Should he do it on his own tonight? After their encounter over the cat bed, Charlie had refused to speak to him for the rest of the evening, so Brad had done the afternoon and evening feedings alone. But then it wasn't like his brother to carry a grudge for long, even when he had good reason. By the time he had gone to sleep and awakened again, everything was usually back to normal. And the sooner that happened, the better Brad would like it.

He bent over Charlie's bed. "Wake up," he whispered, shaking him gently.

Charlie groaned and turned over, burying his face

in the pillow and pulling the sheet over his head. Everything was covered except for a spray of blond hair that always stood up from his crown. "Go away," he ordered, his voice muffled by the pillow.

"Come on, Charlie." Brad sat down on the bed. "Your kitten needs you."

"She's not my kitten," Charlie said, still talking into the pillow. "I don't want her."

Brad laid a hand on Charlie's narrow back. Even through the sheet, he could feel the bumps of his spine. "But you can't pull out, just like that. Besides, we tossed for it. Remember? She's *your* kitten."

"Yeah. We tossed for it," Charlie repeated, flipping over suddenly. "Big deal!"

Brad wasn't sure what Charlie meant — *Big deal!* — but he didn't especially want to ask. "Come on, little brother," he said, giving his arm a playful shake. "You're awake now. Come and help."

But Charlie pulled his arm away and sat up, facing him in the darkness. "I mean it, Brad. She's yours. I don't want a kitten anymore. You can name her and everything."

Brad sighed. "I'm sorry I was rough with you this afternoon. I am . . . really. Sometimes I get so mad at Mom, I could just — " He didn't finish. He didn't know what he could *just* do. The only word that came to mind was cry, and he wasn't about to say that, not to mention do it.

"You didn't hurt me," Charlie replied gruffly.

Brad was so relieved to have his brother's for-giveness that the tears *did* come. At least his eyes stung, and he murmured, "I'll make it up to you. I promise." Then he stood and waited for Charlie to join him.

But Charlie didn't move. Moonlight seeping through his window bleached the color from his skin. Even the golden-brown of his freckles seemed to have been washed away in the watery light.

"Charlie?" Brad asked. "You're coming, aren't you?"

Charlie shook his head.

"Why not?" Brad lowered himself slowly to the side of the bed again. "I thought — "

"Because" — Charlie ducked his head and grabbed a handful of sheet, as if for protection — "I don't like cheats."

Brad's skin went hot, then cold, then hot again. "What do you mean?" His voice rose into a broken squeak at the end of the question.

"I mean you cheated on the toss. 'Heads I win. Tails you lose.' " He said it in a high, mimicking voice, as though that were the way Brad had spoken. "Just cause I'm littler than you, you must think I'm really dumb."

Brad let out a long, slow breath. It was the toss Charlie was talking about. Only that. For a minute he had thought that Charlie knew, somehow, about Dad's dresser and about the wallet and the twenty-dollar bill. "When did you figure it out?"

Charlie crossed his arms over his bare chest. He hadn't even bothered to put on pajamas before he'd come to bed and was sleeping in his undershorts. He probably hadn't bathed, either. This family was really going to pot. He said, "I knew right away."

Brad squirmed inside his skin. "Then why didn't you stop me? Why didn't you say something? We could have done the toss again, fair and square."

Charlie shrugged. "I figured you must want Tuxedo real bad. And the other kitten was just as good, anyway. Better, maybe."

Brad's face burned with embarrassment, but still he asked, "Then why get mad now?"

And Charlie replied, "It's not the toss. It's" — he went silent for a moment, and when the final word came, it was a whisper — "everything. Don't you see?"

Brad didn't see. At least, he didn't want to see. Ice was gathering in the exact center of his chest, and he pressed a hand there, trying to melt it. "Everything?" he asked.

"Like having a brother who's going to end up in jail."

"Jail? What are you talking about?" Brad almost laughed. Dad would be furious if he found out what had been going on, but he was hardly going to send his own son off to jail!

"You know." Charlie's voice rose.

Brad put a finger to his lips in warning, and Charlie finished only a little more quietly.

"I'm talking about you stealing . . . taking stuff from the store."

Brad felt as though he had been pulled up straight by the hair. "Do you really think I did that?"

Charlie nodded emphatically.

"I didn't, Charlie. I promise. I'd never do anything like that. I'm not about to get in trouble with the police. I paid for everything I brought home. Everything!"

"Even the bed?"

"Especially that!" He thought of old Mr. Thorp at the hardware store down the block. He always watched any kids who came in as though he expected them all to be thieves. Brad wouldn't have *dared*. He wouldn't have even considered it, actually.

"Then where — "

But Brad couldn't answer that. "Never mind." He stood again, abruptly. The words came out rough and strong, as though he had a right to be angry at being accused. But how could he explain that he had paid for everything with money he had stolen from their father . . . as though stealing from Dad were better than stealing from the store? On an impulse, he added in an offended tone, "If you don't trust me...."

At first he thought Charlie was going to come around, despite everything. But he just sat up straighter, leaning forward to peer into Brad's eyes, until Brad finally had to turn away, unable to take any more of the scrutiny.

"You're the one who wanted a kitten so bad," Charlie said softly. "So take her. She's yours." And he dropped back into the bed, turned toward the wall, and jerked the sheet up over his head again.

For a moment, Brad stood without moving. Was it that easy? The kitten needed them, was dependent on them, so how could Charlie decide to quit? Pull the sheet over his head and forget?

And then, for another moment, he considered confessing everything, admitting that he had been wrong. Maybe Charlie would even have an idea about how he could begin to make it all right.

But he couldn't talk to a lump in the sheet, and it was silly, anyway, to think a little kid would have any more answers than he did. Brad turned and trudged down the hall to the kitchen, his feet weighted with lead.

CHAPTER
TEN

Brad stood on the concrete patio, waiting for his eyes to adjust to the surrounding blackness. Why was it that nights were so much darker when you were alone?

Not that he needed an eight-year-old with him to keep from being scared.

Heat still radiated from the concrete patio, but when he stepped into the grass, the cool dampness oozed through the canvas of his sneakers. He shivered slightly and, holding the cup of warm milk and the medicine dropper carefully, started toward the looming blackness in the corner of the yard that was the shed.

Was it knowing himself to be a thief that made the world suddenly seem dangerous? If he could steal, and from his own father, then who could be trusted?

The shed took on something of its familiar shape as he drew closer. Still, the overreaching oak tree just behind it swallowed so much of the light that he had to reach out a hand to make the corner solid with a touch. Once he had made contact, he moved along the side, feeling his way toward the door.

"Dark is just the absence of light," his father had told him once. "Things are no different in the night than they are in the day." But though Brad knew, of course, that what his father said was true, and had even repeated the words to himself at moments like this, it had never helped, somehow. The world still *felt* different when the light was taken away.

Like now. The solid blackness that confronted him when he pushed the door open made it seem as though he were about to step into a void. One into which he might fall and fall without ever reaching any kind of bottom.

He located the flashlight on the shelf and clicked it on. The beam of light stabbed through the darkness revealing a pair of round, shining eyes and a half-dark, half-light face. A pair of round eyes and glinting teeth and a pink mouth opened to hiss. Cat was back! She had returned to kill the remaining kitten.

Brad jerked, and the cup in his hand jerked, too. Warm milk slopped onto his arm and the front of his shirt.

His first impulse was to run, to leave the shed and Cat behind and scurry back to his comfortable bed.

He couldn't bear to see another torn scrap of fur that used to be a kitten.

But something kept him from moving, as though his feet were attached to the floor. If he were lucky — if he and the kitten were both lucky — there might yet be time to rescue the tiny creature. He didn't know how Cat had gotten in here. The door had been tightly closed. But however she had come in, maybe she had just arrived and hadn't yet had time to do anything bad.

Brad steadied the beam of the flashlight on the cat.

"Go!" he ordered, remembering, even in his panic, to keep his voice down so that it wouldn't carry to the house. "Shoo! Get out of here!"

Cat rose to her feet, her head lowered, her back arched, and growled, but she didn't move. Brad could make out the tiny, mottled baby curled in the straw beneath her, well away from the new bed. The kitten seemed all right, but he couldn't be sure.

He remembered the soft weight of her in his hand, her eager sucking at the dropper. "You can't have this one!" he cried, and setting the cup of milk and the dropper on the shelf, he lunged to seize the mother. He didn't care if he got clawed, bitten, torn open himself. He'd get her out of here.

Before he could touch her, however, Cat was gone, jumping for the broken pane in the high window. She reached the sill in a single leap, hung suspended for a second or two, her back paws scrabbling against the rough wall, then pulled herself over and out.

"Shoo!" he cried, quite unnecessarily as he could already hear her crashing through the bushes. "Get out of here!"

And then, trembling, his heart banging against his ribs, he turned slowly to shine the flashlight into the corner where he had glimpsed the kitten a moment before. Was she all right?

When the beam picked out the mottled coat and the tiny, reflecting eyes, the creature mewed. No cry had ever been more welcome. Brad dropped to his knees and took her tenderly into his hands. There was no blood. There wasn't even a scratch. The kitten, his kitten, was whole and alive!

He ran his finger gently from her round head down the fragile-feeling spine to her tail. Then he stroked her again. "See," he crooned. "See. You're okay. I got here just in time to save you. That nasty mother didn't get a chance to hurt you."

As if to reassure him, the kitten lifted her head and focused her gray-blue eyes on his face. Brad kissed her minuscule nose.

"I'm here," he told her. "There's nothing to worry about now, baby. I'm here."

But when he settled into the straw and offered her the dropper, she turned away, letting the milk dribble from the corners of her mouth. He couldn't help but notice that her stomach was already round and full.

Had he given her too much at the last feeding? Or hadn't he helped enough then with her elimination?

Surely it wasn't possible that Cat had come back to feed her kitten. Was it? Or that, when they had left the shed unguarded, she could have returned other times?

It had never occurred to him that a cat could jump so high . . . or get in and out through so small an opening. Nor had it occurred to him to think that a mother who had killed one kitten might return to care for another.

But if she had never meant to hurt this kitten, then everything he had done — the constant feedings, getting up in the night, the stealing — had been to no purpose. And that was too much even to think about.

Brad stood, the kitten still cupped in his hand, and peered through the broken pane. The moon seemed to be floating just beyond the branches of the oak tree, pale and full. He lifted his face to its cool light and stroked the kitten.

The moon reminded him of the hot-air balloon he and Charlie had gone up in with their mother. Dad hadn't wanted her to take them. He had said it was too expensive. He had also said she was being "irresponsible" to subject her sons to "such unnecessary danger." *She* had said Dad was a "stick in the mud," and they had gone.

The three of them had floated over patches of greening woods, along a silvery snake of a river, past lakes that looked like shining puddles. The gas burner that kept the balloon inflated had roared and gone silent, roared and gone silent again. And he and Charlie and Mom had peered down at a black bug of a car that scurried along the gravel roads in a flurry of dust, pursuing their sliding shadow. Dad had refused to go up with them, but he had insisted on being at hand when they landed.

Brad could remember it all so clearly. Mom's eyes were alive with light, and she flung out her arms, gathering her sons to her sides. "See," she cried, turning away from the scuttling car, "isn't the world glorious?"

And it was, right up to the moment when they bumped down in the middle of some farmer's stubbled field. Then, before the pilot could pour the champagne, the traditional celebration of such a flight, Dad was there, breathless and cross. "Well, I hope you've gotten that out of your system," he had said, and the shadows had rushed to fill their mother's eyes again.

There had been no shadows the day Brad and Charlie had visited her in her tiny apartment. There was a deep fatigue and something that looked very much like fear, but her eyes had shone still.

For the first time it occurred to Brad to wonder, what would happen if he and Charlie won their campaign? What if they brought her home? Would the light go out for good?

Surely, though, such a question was no concern of his. He was only a kid. Didn't he have a right to have two parents who lived at home and cared about him?

Brad searched the moonshadows and the summer stars for some kind of answer. It took him a few seconds to realize that the darkest shadow cast across the window had just shifted and that the twin stars he had picked out were gleaming eyes. Cat had returned to the sill outside the window and was watching *him*.

"Get out of here!" He hit the frame of the window sharply, and the shadow dropped without a sound, disappearing into the darkness as though into a pool of ink.

The hand that held the kitten trembled.

CHAPTER
ELEVEN

Brad woke up in a foul mood the next morning. He was irritable, itchy, ready to pass it on. He was almost sorry that, when they sat down to breakfast, his father never mentioned the things Brad had said at the supper table the night before. In fact, Dad ate his usual bowl of plain oatmeal with skimmed milk — their mother used to call it library paste — and went downstairs to his office without saying anything at all.

Brad was positively bursting. He sat for a while, eating the Cheerios that were his own daily choice for breakfast and listening to Charlie's spoon scraping the bottom of his bowl. Charlie hadn't yet spoken to him this morning, either. He hadn't even looked in his direction. Brad was beginning to feel invisible.

"It's too bad," he said finally, without looking up to see his brother's face, "that you didn't come out with me last night to see your kitten."

"*Your* kitten," Charlie corrected. "I gave her to you."

"Yeah, well . . . whatever. It's too bad you didn't come, anyway. If I hadn't spent so much time trying to talk you into getting up, I might have gotten out there before *she* did."

There was a brief but heavy silence. Just when Brad had decided that Charlie wasn't going to rise to the bait, a small but stolid voice inquired, "Who? What are you talking about?"

"Cat came back last night. Did you know she can get into the shed through the broken pane in the window?"

Again, Charlie didn't reply, but when Brad finally looked up to see if his arrow had missed the mark, it was clear that it had not. Tears were dribbling down Charlie's cheeks. Gunk was running from his nose, too. Obviously he thought that Cat had killed the remaining kitten. Seeing the predictable response wasn't nearly as satisfying as Brad had expected, though, and he would have said, quickly, "We're lucky. She didn't hurt the kitten this time," except for something else. It was the look of absolute loathing on Charlie's face, as though Brad, himself, were the killer of baby kittens.

"Why did you let her?" Charlie cried. "Why didn't you do something? You should have known she could get in!"

Brad's sympathy vanished instantly, along with his desire to tell the truth. "Why didn't *you*?" he demanded to know. "What were *you* doing? Lying there in bed with the sheet pulled over your head. I'm not responsible for — "

But Charlie didn't wait to hear what Brad wasn't responsible for. He didn't wait to finish his bowl of Cap'n Crunch, either. He shoved his chair away from the table and flung himself through the door, bawling again.

Brad stared at his soggy Cheerios, took one up on the tip of his spoon and released it. Why hadn't he told Charlie that his kitten — their kitten, *the* kitten — was unhurt? What was the point, anyway, in setting the little crybaby off?

Charlie hadn't exactly given him time to explain, though. And he was out in the backyard now. All he had to do, if he wanted to know about the kitten, was to check in the shed. He would see that she was perfectly all right. Not that he'd be apt to do that.

Brad shrugged and got up to dump his remaining cereal into the sink. He'd give Charlie a little time to calm down. If he went out there now, the kid was sure to be blubbering. And he'd had enough of that the last two weeks to last him for an eon or two.

He'd have to straighten things out before evening,

though. It was Friday, the day of the call. And if he didn't get Charlie calmed down, the little twerp just might go over to the other side.

All morning Brad didn't have a chance to talk to Charlie. Logan, a friend of Charlie's, came over, and the two boys careened through the house and around the yard, shooting imaginary guns and yelling, "You're dead!" "No, I'm not. I got you first!" As though *dead* were just another game for little kids to play. They got louder and louder, more and more wild until Dad finally stomped upstairs and sent Logan home, saying it was time for lunch, though it wasn't much past eleven. Then, apparently feeling obligated because he had said it was time to eat, he stayed to fix grilled-cheese sandwiches and tomato soup. Brad and Charlie, who had been getting lunch on their own for years, sat down at the table cautiously. The day was already steamy, and hot food was hardly a treat, but neither of them dared to complain.

After Dad went back downstairs to his office, Brad still didn't say anything to Charlie about the kitten. He wasn't sure why he didn't except that Charlie's not knowing was further proof that the kitten was really Brad's, that Charlie couldn't change his mind about what he'd said last night. How could anyone own a kitten he didn't even know was alive?

When Mom came home, she would be sure to see

it that way. When she came home, he would . . . but he didn't know what he would do. He was torn between a vision of running to her, throwing himself at her as though *he* were eight years old, and one of shaking her the way he had shaken Charlie. He could see her head jerk, too, *her* freckles blur. What right did she have, making everyone so miserable?

Brad had finished the kitten's noon feeding and had returned to the house when he heard a commotion in the backyard. It was Charlie again, and Logan must have returned. Charlie wouldn't be doing all that yelling on his own.

"I'll get you!" Brad could hear clearly. "I'm going to get you!"

But when Brad looked out, he saw that Charlie was, indeed, alone and that he seemed to be playing some kind of game. He had dragged the hose back to the corner of the yard and was spraying it up into the old oak tree.

Brad strolled out, curious. It was amazing how little kids could go on playing and making up games, even in the midst of bad things happening.

Charlie had stationed himself at the base of the tree and was aiming the stream into the branches as though he were a fire fighter directing water onto a fire. "Come on," he yelled when he caught sight of Brad. "Help me."

"Help you what?" Brad asked, disdainful of all the

excitement over nothing. Still, he was glad to have his brother speaking to him again.

"It's Cat!" Charlie yelled. "She's come back."

And that's when Brad saw the mottled creature, her ears flared, her eyes narrowed to evil slits, peering down at them from the limb of the tree. Her coat was already wet, so Charlie's aim had been good. But with Charlie stationed at the base of the tree, there was no way she could come down, either to attack or to escape, without getting even wetter.

When Charlie whipped the hose, sending a shining S of water to the limb where she was perched, Cat snarled and sprang for the trunk, moving higher. Charlie pursued her with the stream of water. The soaked creature looked pathetic, both more scraggly and smaller than she had seemed before.

"Charlie!" Brad reached for the hose.

But Charlie jerked away from Brad's grasp and flipped the hose to send out another snake of water. Again he hit his mark, and Cat scurried higher. Some of the water hit the underside of a branch and rained back down on them, too. Brad stepped aside, but Charlie was so intent on his target that he barely seemed to notice the wetting.

"Don't!" Brad commanded. "There's no reason — " He grabbed for the hose again.

In the brief struggle that followed, the spray caught Brad in the face, and he let go. Instantly Charlie aimed into the tree again. "I'll get that bad mother," he shouted. "I'll get that terrible mother." And Cat cried out, a distant wail, and crawled toward the tip of a high branch. The branch swayed and dipped with her every move.

Determined, Brad seized the hose more force-fully — he wasn't going to let Charlie do this! — but just as his hand touched it, the stream reached Cat again, hitting her full in the face.

She didn't cry this time. She just shook her head. Shook her entire body. Shook herself, silently and terribly, off the branch.

Brad yelled, but if Charlie made any sound at all, it was only the gasp of an in-drawn breath.

It seemed as though the tortoiseshell cat fell for a long time, flailing and twisting to get her feet beneath her. It's true, Brad thought, watching her contortions. Cats land on their feet.

But just when she had almost righted herself, she hit a thick branch, halfway down, and ricocheted off again. After that, she quit twisting. She simply fell until she hit the ground full on her side with a soft, but emphatic thud. And lay there without moving.

Charlie moaned and turned away. Brad, suddenly blazing, all the rage of the past weeks climbing into his throat in one hot lump, grabbed a handful of his brother's shirt and jerked him around to face the consequences of his actions.

"You killed her!" he screamed. "*You* did it. *You!*"

Charlie's shoulders slumped, and he dropped the hose, which snaked backwards a few feet and then settled into spraying off in the direction of the rose-bushes. He didn't even try to extricate himself from Brad's grip, though normally nothing made him more furious than to be held against his will. He stood there gaping at the still form lying at their feet, until Brad, no longer able to look at Cat himself, released him. Then Charlie took off running.

"Come back!" Brad yelled. "You can't go now."

But if Charlie heard, he didn't answer. Nor did he slow his pace. He just kept running until he had disappeared around the front of the house. Except for the motionless cat and the diminishing sound of Charlie's feet, slapping against the sidewalk, Brad might have been alone in the world.

Reluctantly, he knelt to examine Cat more closely. She was stretched along the ground on her side, her legs extended as though she were trying to run as well. Her patchy fur was sodden and clumped into "feathers."

But she was breathing. He could see that she was still breathing.

"Dad," he called. "Dad!" And he ran for the house.

CHAPTER
TWELVE

Dr. Cramer's hands moved gently along the cat's body, pressing, probing, but her eyes were on Brad. "Tell me," she asked. "What happened here?"

Brad had already explained it to his father, as best he could, anyway. On their rapid drive to the vet's office, the still figure of Cat wrapped in a towel on his lap, the kitten cupped in his hand, he had even answered the question, "And where did you get food and money for all this?"

After Brad had said in a halting voice, "From the cupboard ... from your dresser ... from your wallet," his father hadn't spoken again. He hadn't even blinked or grunted or given any other indication of having heard the reply. Except for the way his mouth tightened and the sudden spots of red bloomed in his cheeks.

Brad had wished his father would start yelling. Anything would have been better than the tight-mouthed, flushed silence. At least they could begin to get it over with. But you couldn't tell someone you wanted to be yelled at. You had to wait for it to begin.

"She fell out of a tree," he said now to Dr. Cramer, and he tried to explain it all again.

She interrupted once in an impatient voice to ask, "Why didn't you tell your father about the cat?"

"He wouldn't have let us keep her," Brad replied, sliding a glance toward his father. "He would have said my brother and I aren't responsible enough to take care of a pet."

Dr. Cramer lifted her eyebrows in his father's direction, but what that meant, Brad hadn't the faintest idea.

"Let me see the kitten," she said, when Brad had finished the entire recital.

Brad turned the tiny creature over reluctantly. He had run back to the shed at the last minute, for reasons he didn't even understand, and scooped up the kitten, but now, suddenly, he was afraid. What if the vet found something wrong with *her*?

Dr. Cramer probed the kitten, listened to her tiny chest with a stethoscope, then asked, "What's her name?"

"Muddle," Brad replied, without an instant's thought. "Her name is Muddle."

Dr. Cramer laughed. "Well, at least that's appropriate enough. Appropriate for her coat and for her first days in the world, as well."

Even his dad cracked a smile.

But then, immediately, Dr. Cramer looked serious again, and Brad knew that the lecture was about to begin. She would tell him everything he and Charlie had done wrong, beginning with not having protected Tuxedo from his mother. But to his surprise she announced, instead, "It's a difficult thing, keeping an abandoned kitten alive. I'd say you've done an excellent job here. In many ways, a very responsible job." Her eyes met his father's when she said that word, *responsible*.

"I think Cat came back to help a few times," Brad admitted. "I didn't know she was doing it, though."

"But still you fed her every three hours? At night, too?"

"Except for three A.M. The book said we could skip that one."

"And you took care of her elimination, too?"

Brad nodded. He had.

Dr. Cramer looked in his father's direction. "I'd say that's pretty amazing work."

"My brother helped, too," Brad found himself compelled to explain. It was as if after all the lying, the hiding, the stealing, everything had to be entirely aboveboard now. "He helped most of the time, anyway."

Dr. Cramer laid Muddle down next to her mother's belly, and the tiny kitten snuggled in. Cat was beginning to stir, her eyes fluttering, as though she were waking from a long sleep.

Brad glanced at his father to see if he had been taking it all in, everything Dr. Cramer had said about *responsibility,* but Dad still looked pretty serious. After all, Dr. Cramer hadn't asked the crucial question, about where he had gotten the food and the money to accomplish what he had.

But then Dr. Cramer came up with her own hard question. "Did you *see* the mother kill her first kitten?"

Brad swallowed. Talking about this part was almost worse than telling his dad about taking the money. "When we came in, the kitten was already dead ... and half eaten."

"And so you figured the mother had done it."

"Well, what else could have happened?" Brad demanded, more loudly than he had intended.

"The other thing that *might* have happened," Dr. Cramer offered, running a hand down Cat's side again, "in fact, what's quite likely, is that the first kitten died of natural causes. They do ... often. Twenty percent of all litters of kittens and puppies don't survive their first days." She stroked the kitten now. "And when a kitten dies, the mother often eats the carcass to keep her nest clean. It protects the other kittens, you see, since she can't bury her dead."

Brad stood in the midst of the small examination room, letting the words sink in. Was it possible that Cat hadn't killed Tuxedo, that Tuxedo had died "of natural causes" as Dr. Cramer had said? He staggered beneath the weight of the thought.

"I did it wrong," he said, miserably. "I did everything wrong."

Cat chose that moment to lift her head and stare at him out of those peeled-grape eyes.

"Still," Dr. Cramer said softly, "Muddle is here. Whatever you did or didn't do wrong, you brought your kitten through. You've got to give yourself — and your brother — credit for that."

And to Brad's amazement, his father agreed.

Muddle had found a place to nurse, and Cat, though she still looked wobbly, began to lick her kitten. She was clearly coming around.

Dr. Cramer said, "This cat will need observation after a fall like that. And since she seems to be a stray, I think we can assume she's not up on her vaccinations. She should have those for her safety and yours as well. Unless you want me to turn them both over to the Humane Society." This last was directed to his father.

Brad gasped and turned to his father, too, but though the words burned in his throat, he said nothing. What right did he have to ask?

Dad looked at him for a long moment; then he turned back to Dr. Cramer. "We'll leave her here for now," he said. "I'm sure Brad and his brother will want to call in the morning to see how she's doing. If that's all right."

"Of course," Dr. Cramer said. "You might as well leave the kitten, too. Just for now. Her mother seems ready to take over her job."

Then he and his father got back into the car and drove home, more slowly than they had come and more silently, too.

When they pulled into the garage and stopped, Dad continued to sit staring at the blank wall, still gripping the wheel. "You know what you've done wrong, don't you, son?" he asked, finally, turning to face Brad. "You and Charlie, too."

Brad could only nod. So the punishment was coming now. He had no idea what to expect, but he found himself more relieved than frightened.

"If you'd only told me in the beginning," Dad said. "I might have . . ." But then he stopped, perhaps reconsidering what he might have done. "You're not the only one who's been doing things wrong lately," he continued after a long silence. "I never expected . . . well, any of this. Your mother to go. You and Charlie to stay, for that matter. I guess I've been feeling pretty overwhelmed. Kind of sorry for myself, too."

"Do you want us to go live with Mom?" Brad asked. "All the time, I mean?" He had to force the words out. It wasn't only the house he would miss, or the walk to school or the friends nearby, he realized suddenly. It was his father.

"No." Dad shook his head emphatically. "No. But I'll be awfully glad when you guys start talking to your mother again. Going over there, too. Then maybe I won't feel so much like the world's been dropped on my shoulders."

Brad didn't reply. If they still had a choice, he didn't know what he and Charlie were going to want to do. Or what *he* was going to want to do, actually. He did know about Charlie.

His father straightened his back and pulled in a long breath. Then he turned to face Brad squarely. "You know you'll have to repay the money," he said. "Every cent."

Brad nodded. He knew.

"And you know it's more than the money, don't you?"

Brad was so anxious to get it cleared away, everything that he had done these past two weeks, that his words tumbled out, almost too eager: "You mean the food from the cupboard? I'll repay that, too. Maybe I could get a paper route this summer, and — "

"I mean, it's a question of trust, son. We're a family. Without trust, we don't have anything at all."

Brad's sudden rush of plans faded. Yes, he knew about trust. You trusted and trusted, and suddenly, zap, everything you'd trusted was gone.

His father opened the car door and got out. "By the way," he said, leaning inside again. "Where did you say your brother was?"

Brad hadn't said, but he was pretty sure he knew. "I'll go get him," he replied.

Dad reached over and laid a hand on Brad's shoulder. "Tell him I'm ordering pizza for tonight. Okay?"

"Okay!" Brad waited until the warm pressure of his father's hand had been lifted before climbing out of the car.

"And tell him . . ."

Brad turned back, waiting for the rest, but Dad seemed to change his mind about what he had started to say.

"Just tell him about the pizza," he said. "I'll talk to him about the rest later."

Brad nodded, got his bike out of the garage, and headed out. Though it was too early for Mom to be home from work, he was sure Charlie had gone to her apartment. And this time there wouldn't have been anything to stop him from going the whole way.

CHAPTER THIRTEEN

Charlie was sitting on the bottom step of the apartment building, as forlorn-looking a waif as Brad had ever seen. Brad realized, as he leaned his bike against the railing and walked toward the steps, that he hadn't taken a good look at his brother for a long time. His hair was uncombed and stuck out in unwashed clumps. His face was dirty, too. And the T-shirt he was wearing, a castoff of Brad's that had been washed until it was faded and thin, hung down almost to his knees. He looked like a refugee from some war-torn country.

Brad joined him on the step without speaking, and Charlie didn't even look up. But he moved over a little when Brad sat down — away, not closer — and even the patch of bare concrete between them was an accusation.

After a few moments, Brad finally said, "I think she's going to be all right."

"Who?" Charlie looked up at him, blinking.

"Cat. Dr. Cramer, she's the vet, is keeping her overnight, but she said she thinks Cat's all right. The kitten, too."

"The kitten?" Charlie repeated, almost stupidly, and then Brad remembered that he had thought the kitten was dead, too.

"Cat didn't hurt your kitten." He took a deep breath. "Dr. Cramer says she probably didn't kill Tuxedo, either. He just died, and she was trying to clean out the nest. To protect the one left, you know?"

Beneath his constellation of freckles, Charlie paled, but he made no reply. After a few moments, he said only, "I'm going to see Mom. I'm just waiting for her to get home."

"It's not home," Brad objected.

"It is for her," Charlie said.

There was something about Charlie's tone that made it clear it would be pointless to argue, so Brad didn't try. Instead, he added, after a moment, "Dad knows . . . all of it. He wants to talk to you."

"But I didn't — "

"You knew, though. And, besides, it was your kitten."

"*Your* kitten, too."

"Yeah. My kitten, too." And then after a moment,

Brad added, "I'm pretty sure he's going to let us keep her."

"Really?"

Brad nodded. "Cat, too, I think." He remembered those pale green eyes, the mouth opened to hiss. "I don't suppose she will ever be much of a pet, though."

"I guess she belongs too much to herself," Charlie said solemnly.

Brad knew where Charlie's wisdom had come from. Once when they had all been tugging at Mom, Dad wanting one thing, he and Charlie, something else, she had thrown her hands up and cried, "But I belong to myself. Don't you see?"

And of course, Brad hadn't seen.

"Do you remember the balloon ride?" he asked.

"Sure," Charlie said. "It was fun."

"It scared Dad. He was afraid we'd get hurt."

Charlie didn't say anything.

"It scared me, too." Brad leaned over to study an ant marching across the toe of his sneaker. "I didn't want to go."

"Why did you?" Charlie sounded genuinely curious, as though he couldn't understand how anyone could find himself doing something he didn't want to do. But then Charlie was young.

"Because I didn't want Dad to win. Mom seemed so" — he searched for the word, and when he found it, it was ordinary enough — "unhappy all the time. I wanted her to be happy."

How was it that he had known that about his mother, but had never looked at it before? It was as though he couldn't use the word, and without the word, he couldn't really understand.

The ant, a small red one, was clambering over his laces now, moving steadily upward.

Charlie snuffled, then actually took a tissue out of his pocket and blew his nose. "Do you remember the time we went to one of those cut-your-own places for our Christmas tree?"

"Yeah." Brad nodded vigorously. It had been Mom's idea, of course. Dad had been "busy" and hadn't gone with them. She had fallen in love with a gigantic tree right in the middle of the field. "I tried to tell her the tree she picked out was too big, but it was the only one she wanted. It took two men to get it onto the car. Remember?"

"And, then, when we got home, we couldn't get it into the house," Charlie added.

Brad could see the whole scene. The three of them struggling with the enormous tree. No . . . Dad had helped, too. The way it had gotten stuck in the hallway, just at the point they had to negotiate the turn into the living room. The green scuff marks on the walls. The fallen and broken picture on the floor by the time they had backed the tree out of the house again.

"Then Dad took us downtown to buy a little one," Charlie said.

" 'A proper tree,' " Brad added. "The kind everybody else had." Though after their mother's magnificent attempt, the one they had come home with had seemed puny.

Charlie gave a little bounce on the step. "When we got back, Mom had put the big tree up outside, and she was decorating it for the birds and the squirrels."

"And she didn't take it down until spring," Brad added, smiling. Their mother was like that. *Spontaneous* was the word she preferred. *Foolish,* their dad sometimes said. And Brad was, he knew, more like their father. He liked to keep his world under control, to know, always, what to expect.

He even looked more like his dad with his dark, curly hair and pale skin. Someday he'd probably work in front of a computer in some basement office . . . and not even mind. Not much, anyway.

But, still, he needed his mother. Needed, more than anything, her laughter, her fun, her fresh and *spontaneous* ways. And what good would it be to bring her home if that part didn't come with her?

He hadn't understood before. He supposed he hadn't even tried. The day Mom had moved out, he had sworn to make her come back or, failing that, at least to make her sorry.

When she had been packing, Charlie kept bringing her things he thought she'd forgotten. The pan she'd always used to make brownies, Charlie's favorite food in all the world. The game of Monopoly they'd played with her by the hour. Even the family photo album, the one that went back to the time when first Brad, then Charlie, was toothless and bald, the one that went back so far that it showed Mom and Dad both looking happy.

She had barely glanced at the items Charlie had brought, refusing them, one after another, without even seeming to notice that she was refusing her sons. All they had done together, been together. She just kept saying things like, "I've got so little room in my new apartment." And, "I can't be weighed down with so many things."

Brad had thought — in fact, he'd been certain — that *they* were what was weighing her down. It never once occurred to him that she was cleaning her nest, getting rid of a dead marriage, one that would eventually have done damage to them all.

"Do you remember," he asked Charlie, "when she used to dress up like a witch on Halloween, green warts and everything, and wait behind the door to jump out at the trick-or-treaters?"

Charlie laughed. "One little kid got so scared, he wet his pants."

"But, still, they always came back. All the little kids

thought our house was the very best one to come to."

"It was, too," Charlie said.

Brad wondered if Charlie knew that the reason Mom hadn't dressed up last Halloween was that he and Dad had told her it was *juvenile*. "Maybe," he said, "she'll do it again this year. Her apartment could be the most popular stop in town."

"Yeah," Charlie breathed. "And we could dress up, too. And just for that night, maybe we could sneak the kitten in, and she could be the witch's cat."

"Muddle," Brad said. "I named her Muddle."

"Muddle," Charlie repeated.

The red ant had reached the rim of Brad's high-topped sneaker and it was perched there, exploring the air with its tiny feelers. "Wrong mountain, fella," Brad said, taking the insect onto his fingernail and tipping it gently into the grass next to the walk. "When you climb the wrong mountain, you've got to begin at the bottom again."

The ant lumbered off between the blades of grass, as intent on its new journey as it had been on the last. Brad leaned back against the concrete stairs and closed his eyes, waiting.

It was only ten or fifteen minutes later that he heard the car door slam . . . stiletto heels on the concrete walk . . . his brother's rough cry. And then he opened his eyes to see Charlie running toward their mother, his arms reaching. And she was reaching for Charlie, too, her smile as welcoming and radiant and warm as the sun's.

Charlie threw himself at her so hard that she staggered, but she caught herself immediately and wrapped her arms around him, lifting him off the ground. He clung to her like a bear cub climbing a tree.

Brad stood and reached for his bicycle. He might as well get on home and collect that pizza Dad had promised. There was no point in mentioning it to Charlie now. It was clear he would be spending the weekend with Mom.

Brad mounted the bike, pedaled a few turns, and then, not even knowing why he did so, stopped to look back at Mom and Charlie again. Charlie was still clinging, though his feet were on the ground now. And Mom still had her arms wrapped tightly around him, but she was looking past Charlie to him.

"Brad?" she said, and there was a question in her voice that struck him more strongly than any command.

For a moment he stood, immobilized, taking in her hair, the color of winter-bleached grass, and the fanciful scattering of freckles across her nose and cheeks. But mostly he saw her pale eyes, the pleading in them and the fierceness, too. It was all so familiar.

He laid the bicycle gently in the grass and started toward her, walking at first, then running, finally throwing himself, exactly as Charlie had done. He wrapped his arms around them both.

"Mom," he said, breathing the sweetness of her perfume and the musk of his brother's unwashed hair. "Oh, Mom . . . you're here!"

ABOUT THE AUTHOR

MARION DANE BAUER'S highly acclaimed books for young readers include her Newbery Honor Book, *On My Honor; Rain of Fire,* which won the Jane Addams Peace Award; and her well-received Scholastic Hardcover, *Ghost Eye,* which was a Junior Library Guild selection and an American Booksellers Pick of the Lists. She lives in Eden Prairie, Minnesota.